A Dodo at Oxford

The Oxfam bookshop in St Giles, Oxford, where the diary was bought

A Dodo at Oxford

The unreliable account of
a student and his pet dodo

Edited by

Philip Atkins and Michael Johnson

OXGARTH PRESS

2010

Published by Oxgarth Press
30 Finsbury Place, Chipping Norton, Oxfordshire, OX7 5LS
www.oxgarth.co.uk

Oxgarth is a registered trademark

© Michael Johnson 2010

Database right Oxgarth Press (maker)

First edition 2010

British Library Cataloguing in Publication Data.
A catalogue record for this book is available from the British Library.

ISBN 978-0-9534438-2-6

3 5 7 9 10 8 6 4 2

Typeset in Adobe Garamond Premier Pro and Myriad Pro
Printed in the United Kingdom by
T. J. International Ltd,
Padstow, Cornwall

In memory of Philip Atkins, 1950–2009

A NOTE FROM THE EDITORS

This is the story of the remarkable re-emergence of a diary printed over three hundred years ago. We came across it whilst browsing in the Oxfam charity bookshop on St Giles. It claims to be an Oxford student's observations on what may well have been the last dodo to have lived. Sensing something special, we promptly bought it for ninety-five pence.

We should begin by mentioning our concerns about the authenticity of the diary. It looks right to us, but we have not been able to find a record of it in any library catalogue. Sometimes the truth is stranger than fiction, but a word of warning seems to be in order. Indeed the situation brought to mind the supposed discovery of the Hitler diaries which were announced to a frenzy of worldwide interest in April 1983. Extracts were published in *The Sunday Times*, before they were shown to be fakes. Similar literary hoaxes have included diaries supposedly by Mussolini and Jack the Ripper.

We purchased the diary on 5 March 2008, but what of its previous history? We can only go back five days to the Leap Day of Friday 29 February; before that its ownership is unknown. By good fortune a friend was working as a temporary assistant at the bookshop early that morning and remembers the donation of a cardboard box full of books. She was arranging a display of Fairtrade chocolates at the time. Due to her glasses being at the opticians, she only caught a blurred view of the departing donor and heard a deep-toned 'You're welcome!' in reply to her hasty thanks. An hour or so later she carried the box down to the basement. After donning a pair of yellow rubber gloves, she weeded out the unsaleable items, including some copies of a cross-stitch magazine from the 1970s.

Returning from an assertiveness training course on the following Tuesday, the bookshop manager began a detailed sorting of the donations. On investigating a dirty brown paper package tied up with a bootlace, the intriguing little book was discovered. It was battered, fusty, interleaved with a bizarre mixture of additional items, and without its binding. It was put to one side for special valuation. The next day, Wednesday 5 March, the manager was attending a one-day time management and continuous improvement course. It was during her absence that the book was accidentally priced and put in the bargain box just inside the shop's front door. There it sat amongst cookery booklets, bluffer's guides, and joke books, until we saw it.

The excitement at our find led to a desire to print a small quantity of facsimile copies to share with a wider audience. But what if the book had been donated by mistake? We placed an advertisement in the local newspaper *The Oxford Times* on 14 March (shown opposite). However, on the rather wet and windy day no one turned up at the rendezvous apart from a group of American tourists who had lost their guide.

Although we have some doubts about the authenticity of the diary, we have tried hard to provide informative and accurate notes to accompany it. You may also wish to visit our website at www.oxgarth.co.uk. Unfortunately, the rush to publish, as well as a typesetting problem, meant that a few pages have been printed from photocopies that still include our handwritten comments.

Several friends have commented about the suspect nature of the diary, occasionally with a lack of tact, and urged us to show it to experts before going ahead with publication. Perhaps the decision to publish will come to be regretted, but we leave it to the wider world to decide.

The advertisement the editors placed in
The Oxford Times on 14 March 2008
asking for the donor of the
diary to meet them.

Alongside the pages of the diary you will find our comments which we hope will be helpful and interesting.

The diary is reproduced at 100% actual size, to give as accurate an impression of it as possible.

It begins with blank pages, which are known as endpapers (this is because they appear at both ends of a book and are there to help in connecting the cover of the book to the text pages).

There's nothing printed on these pages, but there is a pencil signature that perhaps reads 'H. Hutchison', and has a distinctive looped crossbar on the letter H. It's difficult to put a date to the signature, but we thought it might be from the nineteenth century.

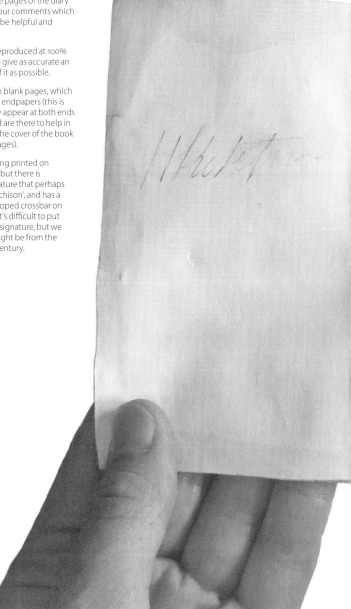

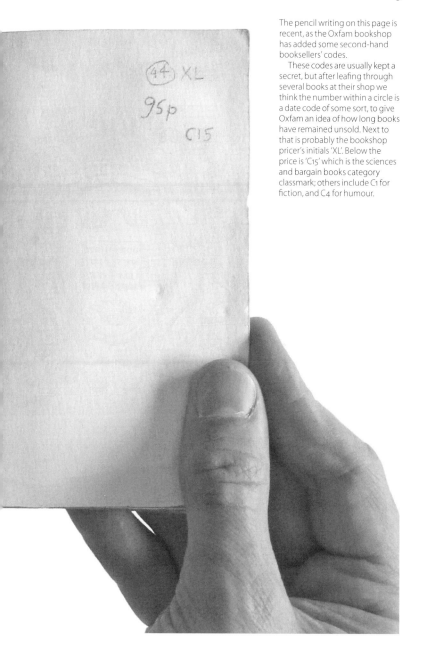

3

The pencil writing on this page is recent, as the Oxfam bookshop has added some second-hand booksellers' codes.

These codes are usually kept a secret, but after leafing through several books at their shop we think the number within a circle is a date code of some sort, to give Oxfam an idea of how long books have remained unsold. Next to that is probably the bookshop pricer's initials 'XL'. Below the price is 'C15' which is the sciences and bargain books category classmark; others include C1 for fiction, and C4 for humour.

The left-hand page is called the frontispiece, and includes such an ornate illustration that the diary must have been thought to be of some importance. The illustration is called the blazon of the University of Oxford coat of arms, and has a delightful definition in heraldic language, as follows:

> Azure upon a book open proper, leathered gules, garnished or, having on the dexter side seven seals of the last, the words 'DOMINVS ILLVMINATIO MEA', all between three open crowns, two and one, or.

And to help you translate:

azure = blue

proper = depicted in natural colours

gules = red

or = gold, or yellow

dexter side = The right side of a shield. But this is from the point of view of the shield and not the viewer, so as we observe it, it is on the left. This follows the same convention that a doctor would use with a patient when removing a leg. It's important to have such systems and understand which way round they work. The other side is called the 'sinister'.

seal = In this case, short leather straps to enable the pages of a book to be fastened shut. That there are seven may be a reference to the seven seals binding the scroll held in the right hand of God in the New Testament's Book of Revelation.

DOMINVS ILLVMINATIO MEA = These Latin words translate as 'The Lord is my light'.

A
BIRD
CONSIDERED

BEING

a Faithful and True RECORD
of the Unique Obſervacions of
that Curious and Exceeding Rare
BIRD of the Tropics, *The Dodo.*

In Five Volumes.
Volume I.

Undertaken by an Oxford Student
after a moſt Comprehenſive
Method, with the RESULTS therof,
Dedicated to Mr A - - - - - -.

OXFORD,
Printed at the THEATER, *A. D.* 1695.

It is a mystery and a disappointment to us that we have failed to find any record of the diary in either the Bodleian Library in Oxford, or the archives of the Oxford University Press.

Harry Carter's *A History of the Oxford University Press*, published in 1975, lists twenty publications for 1695, but not this one.

The title page says that this book is the first volume of five. We've also been unable to track down a record of the other volumes.

If any reader has seen any of the volumes, we would be very interested to hear from them.

The place and date on the title page are called the imprint. The Theatre referred to is the Sheldonian Theatre in the academic heart of Oxford, completed in 1669, and Christopher Wren's first major architectural design. The University's ceremonies, such as the awarding of degrees, were also held there, which meant that the printers kept having to move their equipment out of the way. Ceremonies are still held in the Theatre (as well as concerts), but the printers moved next door to the Clarendon Building in 1713, before moving again in 1830 to Walton Street.

Sheldonian Theatre.

This is the other side of the leaf of paper on which the title is printed, and so is known as the 'title verso'. 'Verso' refers to the left-hand page of an open book (and 'recto' to the right-hand page).

Imprimatur

This is the mark of approval (in Latin *imprimatur*) from the Vice Chancellor of the University of Oxford at the time. Henry Aldrich (1647–1710) was also Dean of Christ Church from 1689, a talented musician, and amateur architect. The Vice Chancellor is the principal administrative officer of the University.

    The curious double year of 2 March 1694/5 is explained in **Appendix 1** at the end of this book.

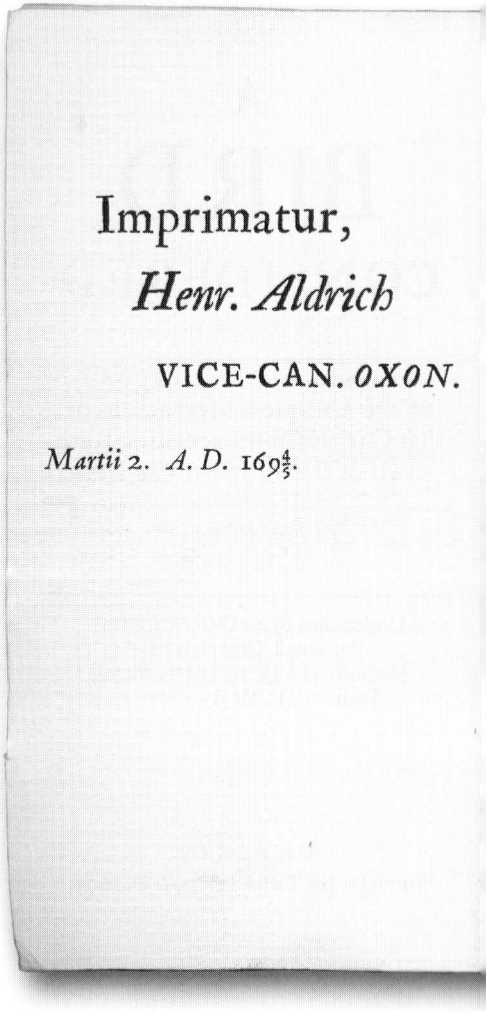

Imprimatur,

Henr. Aldrich

VICE-CAN. *OXON.*

Martii 2. A. D. 169⁴⁄₅.

Thurſday March. xxii. ⚕ 7

at the **Coffee-Houſe** in the morning I heard the **Dutchman** had
been found. I went downe the
High Street to the Bridge at
Magdalen and on the riverbank
there, juſt by the Garden, was a
crowd gathered about his poor
drowned bodye. Many there
could name him as the **Dutchman**
for the **Proctor's** men, ſo I came
away. It was a month ago I met
him often, going about in hope
of finding Lodgings, where he
might exhibit his Menagerie-in-
Miniature; but he was too much
in the Taverns, mad with drink,
and I kept apart from him. Then
he had gone away on his travels
agayne I ſuppoſed.

Missing pages
Unfortunately, it looks like ten pages from between the title verso page and page 7 of the diary are missing. It seems that they were deliberately torn out—a great shame as we are forced to begin halfway through an entry.

There is little way of knowing who might have done this, why, and at what stage in the book's life (**Appendix 7** has a related discussion about the missing pages).

If you would like to follow the Oxford locations mentioned in the diary, please refer to the maps in **Appendix 10**.

ſ The long s character is often used in the diary, but takes a bit of time to get used to reading if you have not seen it before.

When this diary was printed there were two forms of a small letter s. One version was the s shape we use today, and the other is called the long s and looks like this: ſ. The long s was used at the beginning, or in the middle of a word; whereas the short s appears at the end of a word. **Appendix 3** gives more information about the long s, as well as some entertaining examples to get you up to speed.

In the page above, the words using the long s are:

Thurſday → **Thursday**,
houſe → **house**,   juſt → **just**,
ſo → **so**,   ſuppoſed → **supposed**

8   *Friday March.* xxiii.

After a night without sleepe, seeing his corpse agayne before me in my fevered imaginings, I understood that now the Bird he gave me for safe-keeping is mine to keep. What became then of the Singeing Mice, and the Arithmeticall Fleas? Drowned in his pockets no doubt. With no name and no-one to claim him he will be given over to the Students and dissected upon the slab.

Events have turned out as you might have wished, *said Mr. Sawyer*. Are you sure it was not you who did away with him? And will you keep the Bird for your Pet? *enquired Mr. Flay*. I told them I would keep it and care for it, all the while making good observacions

Mr Flay and Mr Sawyer
This is our first introduction to Mr Flay and Mr Sawyer, two of the principal characters in the diary.

Catchword 'observacions'
Old books often included the first word of a page at the bottom of the preceding page. If you are reading the text out loud it reduces the jump between pages, and also confirms that the pages are in the right order.

Friday March. XXIII.   9

obfervacions to difcover its true Nature. It is but a forry fat lump of a Bird, *faid Mr. Sawyer*. It is the freekifh iffue of a Turkie and a Goofe, *faid Mr. Flay*. I told them it was brought from an Ifland in the far Southern Ocean, called *Mauritius*, where its like were maffacred by Sailors for food; it was likely one of the laft of its kind to be alive, there was not another in all England to be feen, or in Europe. So faid the Dutchman, *faid Mr. Sawyer*. But I think my friends have begun to look upon my Dodo with new eyes.

B

The Island of Mauritius

The diarist's discussion with his two friends, Mr Sawyer and Mr Flay, shows that he had some reliable knowledge of Mauritius, where the dodo lived. The island is in the Indian Ocean, off the south-east coast of Africa, and was probably first visited by Arabs several centuries before the Portuguese and Dutch in the sixteenth century.

The Portuguese name for the dodo was *Valghvogel*, which translates as 'disgusting bird', following their experiences of eating them. It was probably the rats, pigs, and monkeys that the European visitors brought to Mauritius that eventually caused the extinction of the dodo by making short work of the eggs in the birds' unprotected nests.

It is unclear when exactly the dodo became extinct, but current research suggests that it was probably by the 1640s. So our student's notes in the diary could be the last record of a living dodo (**Appendix 2** discusses in which year our student was writing). Benjamin Harry, the first mate on an English ship which visited Mauritius in 1681, mentions the dodo, but this may well be a confusion with the Mauritius red rail.

Page signature 'B'
At the foot of this page is one example of several page signatures that appear in the diary. For more information see **Appendix 7**.

10

Served at college
The last sentence of this entry could be a clue to our diarist's way of life at this time. Perhaps he was a servitor, a lower order of student who subsidized his education at an Oxford college by performing menial tasks—waiting at table, lighting fires—for higher status students. Mention of a landlord, however, suggests that our diarist is not living in college and so not a student at all, just a servant. But are 'my studies' the observations of dodo he has begun, or something else?

10   *Saturday March.* xxiv.

At my Studies all the morning. Dodo tries to catch a flie at the window. *Queſtion :* is this ſport, or hunger? Thus far it will eat all kinds of food, whatever is offered. It makes a prodigeous meſs about my Room, which I muſt ſpend much time in cleaning, ſo that my friends will continue to viſit and my Landlord be not angered. He knows nothing of Dodo and I mean to keep it ſecret. The Maid is in our confidence. Served at College to Mr. Twiſſe.

f Don't forget that **Appendix 3** gives more information about the long s.

Sunday March. xxv. ☉ ♋ **11**

Mr. Ned Tompkyns viſited after Chapel to make Sketches of Dodo. I have requeſted theſe to be done ſo that I may ſhew them to Mr. Aſhmole and perſuade him, by their livelineſs, of the poorneſs of the ſtuffed Bird in his Rarities. He will ſee it is too ſtooped, as if ſat upon, and ſhabby beſides. But I will not diſcloſe to him I have a living Bird; he would ſurely want it for himſelf.

B 2

Following the date are a couple of strange-looking symbols. The first one must represent a phase of the moon, and the second is a sign of the zodiac. See **Appendix 4** for more information.

New Year's Day
The 25 March used to be the first day of the new year, but the diarist doesn't mention it. See **Appendix 1** for more information about time.

Mr Ned Tompkyns
Ned Tompkyns, the artist, joins Mr Flay, Mr Sawyer, the maid, and our nameless diarist in the cast of regular characters.

Elias Ashmole
Elias Ashmole (1617–92) was a larger-than-life figure who will play a significant part in the life of our diarist. The reference to 'his bird' is undoubtedly to a stuffed one, which is very likely the bird from the Tradescant collection inherited by Ashmole. The surviving head and foot of that stuffed dodo have stayed in Oxford until the present day, and are now on show at the University Museum of Natural History. The Ashmolean Museum and the University Museum of Natural History both have special displays of some of the surviving items from the Tradescant Collection.

Swallowing stones

The dodo certainly swallowed stones, as early hunters soon discovered when they butchered the bird for the pot. Many birds, crocodiles, and seals swallow grit or stones to aid digestion. It is believed that some dinosaurs also did this. Birds do without teeth but have a muscular grinding organ, called the gizzard or *ventriculus*, as part of their digestive tract. It is lined with a horny layer which, with the assistance of the grit, breaks up hard food such as seeds as it passes through on its way to the stomach.

Ostriches

There were indeed ostriches kept by King Charles II at Whitehall Palace in the 1670s. In 1682 the Moroccan ambassador made a gift of 'Lions and Estridges' to King Charles II. The lions went to the Tower of London menagerie and the ostriches to join other exotic birds in St James's Park.

12   *Monday March*. xxvi.

Dodo has a payneful crye. It is worſe than a Peacocke, *ſaid Mr. Sawyer*, and toſſes his hat over the Bird's head; which ſtrange to tell ſilences it in an inſtant, and it will ſtand ſtill and dumb as a Statue for upward of an hour, until the hat is taken off. Its voice is quite various. One kind of utterance is a ſoft babbling, like babye-talk as it ſettles in its baſket to ſleepe.

The King I hear has an Oſtrich-Bird at Whitehall. Theſe Birds alſo take ſtones into their ſtomacks. *Queſtion*: Is the Dodo a ſmall Oſtrich?

Squashed between the pages

An unfortunate eight-legged arthropod of the order *Araneae*, otherwise known as a spider, appears above. Despite bearing several pairs of eyes, the ability to spin silk into wondrous webs, and a pair of venomous fangs, this one wasn't quite quick enough to escape. We think it might be a House spider (*Tegenaria duellica*), but was it trapped in the seventeenth century, or more recently? It looks fairly fresh.

Tuesday March. xxvii. ♌ **13**

I will endeavour to preferve Dodo's voice, in cafe by ill fortune it fhould die. A voice is the vital fpirit of a Creature. Firftly, I fhall match it on my Reed-Pipe and play it over to Mr. Foffik, Mufic Scolar at Magdalen College, fo that he may write it as notes. Secondly, I will fpell out the founds as words. Thirdly, I will tap on my Tambour the rythemicall pattern. Combined thefe Methods will be fair Record. Alas, my friends ridicule my efforts with applaufe, bravo, encore, &c. *Queftion:* Why does a Bird finge, and what need is there for fuch varietie of fong?

B 3

Bird song

If you want to explore the fascinating subject of bird song—how it has inspired poets and composers, challenged scientists to record it, analyse and understand it, and even led one man to write a two hundred page book on a three-note song—*Why Birds Sing* by David Rothenberg, 2005, is a good place to start.

Our diarist's efforts to transcribe the dodo's song follow the entry for 4 April.

Dreams

Attitudes to dreams in the seventeenth century ranged from superstition to philosophical speculation. The girl who wanted to know the identity of her future husband had to sleep in another county and tie her left garter around the stocking of her right leg while repeating certain verses with each knot:

> This knot I knit
> To know the thing, I know not yet,
> That I may see,
> The man that shall my husband be.

A bubbling scum

Some thought dream interpretation was a dangerous political and spiritual habit, and that dreams were a symptom of madness or drunkenness.

Thomas Nashe wrote that they were 'nothing else but a bubbling scum or froth of the fancy, which the day hath left undigested'. René Descartes suggested the possibility that what seemed to be waking life may be all a dream, and how difficult it was to prove otherwise. The scientist Thomas Willis, dissecting brains, sought to remove sleep and dreams from the realm of the supernatural. He saw the natural spirits of man, needing to rest, being locked into the brain while he slept, and dreams were the result of a few spirits escaping and wandering through the brain, doing mischief.

Dream visions continue to be used as an allegorical device in literature, in the tradition of Dante's *Divine Comedy*, Langland's *Piers Plowman*, and John Bunyan's *Pilgrim's Progress*.

---

14 *Wedneſday March.* xxviii.

Mr. Flay amuſes us with an account of his ſtrange Dreame. I will record it as Dreames are of intereſt: I believe they declare Man's Temperament to Himſelf. I ſaw, *he ſaid*, figures ſtanding at a corner under a bright light, their faces hidden by Hoodes, each holding in one hand a ſnuff or jewell-box, open, and looking into it, or ſometimes poring what was in it into their ear. They wore dark clothing, looſe-fitting, white boots, and a ſtripe ran downe their breeches. Of what ſex theſe people might be was impoſſible to diſcover, and no voice could be heard.

Diary dreams

The dreams mentioned on this page and later on are some of the most remarkable aspects of the diary. However, we have decided not to comment on them and restrict our marginal notes to historical material. We leave the reader to make what they can of them.

Thurſday March. xxix. ♍ 15

I am a Maſter of the Hunt, *ſaid Mr. Sawyer*, and can imitate the Calls of twenty Birds to lure them in. He proceeded to trye them with Dodo. The Bird ſhewed no intereſt. So he tryed : the barking of a Dog, the roaring of a Lion (he ſaw one at the Tower), the howling of an Ape (likewiſe), the hiſſing of a Snake, and more beſides, getting downe upon his haunches in fierce faſhion. Dodo was untroubled, tho' my Landlord called up the ſtair in ſome alarm to know what was amiſs, and the Experiment was concluded. *Theoria :* the Dodo knows no fear, or is ſtupid.

B 4

All kinds of creatures

A Royal Menagerie was begun at the Tower of London in the thirteenth century, possibly in 1235, when the Holy Roman Emperor, Frederick II, presented Henry III with a wedding present of three leopards.

By the sixteenth century it was sometimes on view to the public. King James I set up baiting spectacles, pitting dogs, bulls, and bears against lions. By the eighteenth century visitors were allowed to feed their pet dog or cat to the lions in lieu of the price of admission. The last animals left in 1835 and were transferred to the new Zoological Gardens in Regent's Park, now known as the London Zoo.

Dwarf Gibson

Richard Gibson (called Dwarf Gibson, 1605 or 1615?–1690) was a successful miniature painter in the service of Philip Herbert, Fourth Earl of Pembroke, the Lord Chamberlain. He was also employed at the court of King Charles I, where he met his future wife, Anne Sheppard, also a dwarf. Their marriage, on St Valentine's Day 1641, was one of the last great festivities before the descent into Civil War.

Richard and Anne had five surviving children, all of average stature, at least three of them active in the art of miniature painting. At the Restoration, Gibson was briefly king's limner to King Charles II (a limner is another term for a portrait painter). He then took up the post of drawing master to the two daughters of James, Duke of York, Mary and Anne. He stayed with them for a while in Holland, before returning to London in 1688 with Mary, by then the wife of William of Orange.

16   *Friday March*. xxx.

Coming in from my Walk I find Mr. Tompkyns at his Draweing but getting on so slowely and so daintilie I can see no progress; he is more lively in his rubbing-out. He interrupts my studies with his talkativeness. I was Pupil to Mr. Gibson, *he said*, who was Portrait Painter in Miniature to the late King. He was a Dwarf, and made sometimes to jump out of a cake at table to surprise His Majestie's guests. I think Mr. Tompkyns is more used to the flattering and frivolity of Court than the true studie of Nature for Science.

There appears to be a tea stain on the diary page above, perhaps the impression from the bottom of a cup.

Saturday March. XXXI. ○ ♎ **17**

With Mr. Flay to Chrift Church Meadow, to affift him in the learning of his Difputation. It is too fancifull I fear for thefe fhouting-matches and requires much amendement.

I am diftracted by my Dreame, *he faid,* of a travelling houfe in darknefs. The Building was two ftoreys high, lit up infide like a Lanthorn, and the people infide were fitting all in rows as if they were at a meeting, looking out at me as they paffed by. The houfe caft a great light before it.

Why does the pencil sketch include horses? There are none in Mr Flay's description.

The signs following the diary date are a full moon and the zodiac sign for Libra (see **Appendix 4**).

Christ Church Meadow is shown on the map in **Appendix 10**.

Disputations
These were tests of a student's command of logic, rhetoric, and grammar, as well as Latin and Greek prose and poetry. They were staged in public, either for examining degree candidates or honouring visiting dignitaries, and were considered the pinnacle of accomplishment. Sometimes the subjects chosen were topical and other times more hypothetical, for example 'Is the Moon habitable?'.

A participant, called the respondant, first offered an answer or interpretation of the question for disputation, and advanced arguments to support it. Next an opponent, or opponents, stated contradictory propositions, and attacked flaws in the respondant's reasoning. Finally the moderator, or determiner, summed up the arguments, pro and con, pointed out fallacies in the reasoning, called attention to arguments that had been overlooked, bestowed praise or blame, and handed out the 'determination'. Full dress disputations took place at important academic occasions, for the edification and entertainment of visitors. It was a stylized debate with fixed rules, usually less about determining truth than a kind of verbal duel using memorized arguments.

18

This monthly table is an impressive demonstration of the diarist's earnest study of the dodo.

Weight

How was the dodo weighed? By taking it to some public scales in Oxford, or perhaps the diarist had some in his room? Did it have to be put in a cloth bag first, or did it perhaps go willingly?

Food

On Mauritius the dodo feasted on a plentiful supply of high-energy fruit that fell almost year round from the many different palm trees. During times of plenty it gorged itself, storing up fat reserves for any periods of scarcity. This banquet, and the lack of any predators, seems to have led the bird down an evolutionary path of many thousands of years until it was the big, plump, flightless, and trusting bird encountered by the European voyagers who first landed on the island at the end of the sixteenth century.

Which particular fruit the dodo favoured is uncertain because of the disappearance of most of the island's original habitat, although its formidable beak suggests it had the ability to break into anything tough-skinned. There were reports of the dodo wading into shallow waters, so might it have included fish and crustaceans in its diet?

March.

Monthly Digeſt of Obſervacions

Weight	34 pounds and increaſing to 37 pounds
Height	16 inches with head up
Length	12inches beak to tail
Food	A frog, cobnuts, apples (many), crab apple, bread (any), raſpberry jellie, damſon cheeſe, cowſlips, muſtard ſauce, eggs (boyled), chub, eel, tenche, horſe muſhroom, champignon (dried), butter, beetle, a candle.
Moult	none but ſome downe
Stones	As many as were given, ſmall, and gravel, and coins, a buckle.

March.

Sleepe	As soon as it grows dark, or when its head (or eyes alone) is covered, after food, in warm sun or fireside, when petted, during music, when alone.
Activitie	Little within the room. Mr. Sawyer took it to the Country one time, but it was nearly lost for surprising speed of running. About as fast as Mr. Sawyer can run.
Responsive-ness	none

Activity

But how fast a runner was Mr Sawyer? Perhaps this dramatic incident occurred during the time covered by the missing pages?

A blank diary page, see **Appendix 11**.

The Mallard

It is interesting that a mallard is one of the birds chosen for comparison in the engraving, as All Souls College in Oxford has it as its emblem. Legend tells that when the foundations for the college were being dug in the fifteenth century the duck flew up out of a drain. Ever since it has been celebrated twice a year in the singing of a mad song, never to be heard by a stranger's ears. Here is a sample verse:

Dodo with other Feathered Birds to Compare.

Pag. 21.

Turkey.   Mallard.   Ayleſbury Duck.

Dodo.

Chicken.   Pigeon.   Gooſe.

G. Higginbottom delin.   M. Burghers ſculp.

This image is printed using the intaglio process from a copper engraving. Ink is transferred to the paper from the recesses in the copper plate. The text on the other pages of the diary is printed by a different process, called letterpress, in which ink sits on the top of the metal letters before being impressed into the paper.

In 2002 a team lead by Dr Beth Shapiro of Oxford University reported on their testing of DNA samples taken from the bill of the dodo preserved in the Oxford University Museum of Natural History. They proved that the bird was a kind of pigeon and that its closest surviving relative is the Nicobar pigeon.

Who is the G. Higginbottom that has signed the copper-engraving? Is it the Guy who is mentioned later in the diary?

On page 73 there is another copper-engraving and a note about Michael Burghers, the engraver.

The Griffin, Bustard, Turkey, Capon,
Let other hungry mortals gape on,
And on their bones with stomach full hard,
But let All Souls men have their Mallard

And the chorus is:

O by the blood of King Edward,
O by the blood of King Edward,
It was a swapping, swapping Mallard.

'Swapping' is an old word which seems to mean either big, or flapping, or hacking as with a weapon.

Every one hundred years, on All Souls Day (2 November) the Fellows of the college perambulate the grounds at night with torches, even onto the roof, led by Lord Mallard carried in a sedan chair, singing the song and carrying a dead duck on a pole. They return to the common room in the small hours for a final drink, this time laced with the duck's blood. The next occasion will be in 2101.

22

This drawing is in blue ink, probably done relatively recently using a felt-tip pen. It seems to be in the same style as the drawing on the diary page for 5 April. There are three faces, which seem to look either happy or quizzical. How did this diary fall into the hands of a child so keen to practice their drawing skills?

Felt-tipped pens ...
The first felt-tipped pens were made in the 1940s from coarse wool felt. These were largely superseded by the invention of the modern fibre-tip pen in 1962 by Yukio Horie of the Tokyo Stationery Company. Since then further developments have been made using fine nylon and other synthetic fibres ground to a point. The ink is fed to the tip of the pen from a soft fibrous reservoir being drawn by capillary forces. These same forces pull the ink out onto the surface of the pen tip and then onto the paper.

... and biros
The other great development at this time was the ballpoint pen, or biro. In 1938 the first workable pen with a rolling ball was designed by two Hungarian brothers, Ladislao Biro, a journalist, hypnotist, and painter, and his older brother Georg Biro, a chemist. The Biros emigrated to Argentina during World War II and began to produce pens there in 1943. Henry Martin began manufacturing Biro pens in England for use by Royal Air Force pilots as it was the only pen that would not leak at high altitudes. In 1945 Baron Marcel Bich

began manufacturing ballpoint pens in Paris, soon producing over seven million 'Bic' pens a day.

23

Sunday *April.* 1.

There is precious little Draweing from Mr. Tompkyns but he is companie for Dodo (and affifts in eating my fcant provifions). I was at College to reftore Rooms broken up by revellree. Mr. Sawyer came to vifit with a fore head and in handling the Bird roughly, to determine its fex, he received a wound. He is impreffed by Dodo's growing plumpneffe, and imagines how he would carve it. I cannot work in fuch turmoyle and noyfe, *faid Mr. Tompkyns*, and put afide his work agayne. Yefterday the Bird fnatched off Mr. Tompkyn's Eye-Glaffes and broke them, fwallowing a Lens whole.

23

This is the opening page of a new month. The ornaments are made up from combining single units together. These were bought by John Fell at the same time as the typefaces acquired in the seventeenth century. See **Appendix 9** for more information.

By now we can perhaps safely assume that Mr Flay and Mr Sawyer are students.

April Fool's Day

April Fool's Day is traditionally the occasion for playing tricks. It dates back many centuries and originated in France as the *poisson d'avril*, literally 'April Fish'. One trick involves attaching a fish to the back of an unsuspecting person. However, the earliest known April Fool's Day trick is to send the victim from one conspiring person to another, with each one further elaborating the fool's errand. One of the first mentions of this version of the trick in England appears in Thomas Dekker's *Seven Deadlie Sinnes of London* published in 1606.

Animal Behaviour

The diarist seems to be anticipating by over two hundred years the branch of science that came to be known as Comparative Ethology. For a long time the behaviour of animals was better understood by farmers, hunters, and enthusiastic amateurs than by scientists who concentrated their attention on classification and anatomy, studying preserved museum specimens. It was not until the pioneering work of the outstanding naturalists Konrad Lorenz (1903–1989) and Niko Tinbergen (1907–1989) that the importance of studying creatures in their natural environments began to be understood.

24   *Monday April.* 11. ♍

My firſt Experiment is begun, to diſcover if there is the Power of Reaſon in my Bird. Taking three boxes of like ſize, and without their lids, I drew Signes upon them, viz : a Croſs, a Circle, and a Square. In ſecrecy I put an Apple under the Circle box. Dodo came foreward, and knowing I will often hide food for it to ſearch out at certayne times, ſoon went to the boxes and knock'd them aſide, thereby getting the Apple. I put up the boxes agayne as before but in a different order, the Apple agayne under the Circle. Repeating this proceedure over many times, and at the coſt of many Apples I can ill afford, the Bird being ſo quick to eat them up, I was at the concluſion ſure

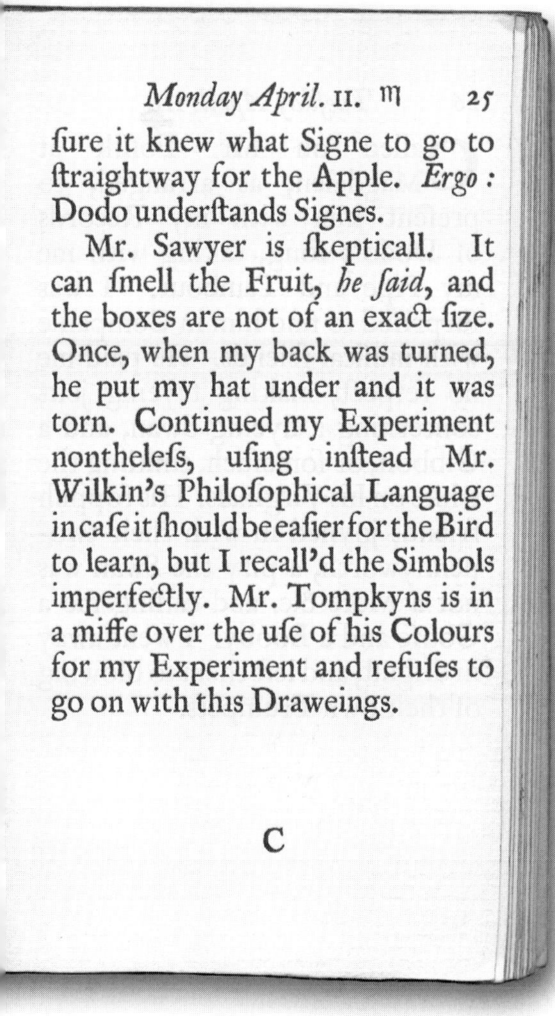

Monday April. 11. ♏ 25

fure it knew what Signe to go to ftraightway for the Apple. *Ergo :* Dodo underftands Signes.

Mr. Sawyer is fkepticall. It can fmell the Fruit, *he faid*, and the boxes are not of an exact fize. Once, when my back was turned, he put my hat under and it was torn. Continued my Experiment nonthelefs, ufing inftead Mr. Wilkin's Philofophical Language in cafe it fhould be eafier for the Bird to learn, but I recall'd the Simbols imperfectly. Mr. Tompkyns is in a miffe over the ufe of his Colours for my Experiment and refufes to go on with this Draweings.

C

Mr Wilkins

This must be John Wilkins (1614–1672), educated at Magdalen College, Oxford, and then Warden of Wadham College, Oxford. He later married Oliver Cromwell's youngest sister, Robina, and was a leading figure in the group of intellectuals that founded the Royal Society.

His *Essay towards a Real Character and a Philosophical Language* of 1668 proposes a new kind of shorthand using approximately 3,000 symbols representing all things and ideas. This was inspired by the idea of a universal language, used by Adam in Paradise, and later by all the people of the world, until it was lost. Wilkins claimed it could be learned in one month, and be understood by anyone, irrespective of their native language, and would have particular use in missionary work . It was not a success, but is considered a pioneering study in semantics. An example is shown below.

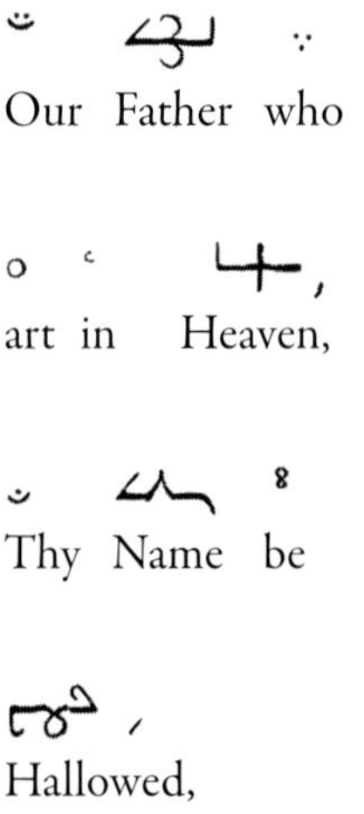

Our   Father   who

art   in   Heaven,

Thy   Name   be

Hallowed,

WHAT'S THIS?
REPLACE WITH
A SWAN!

This must be a reference to the madrigal *The Silver Swan*, by Orlando Gibbons (1583–1625), one of the greatest of early English Composers, based on the ancient fable of the swan that sings most sweetly before its death.

The silver swan, who
living had no note,
When death approach'd,
unlock'd her silent
throat;
Leaning her breast
against the reedy shore,
Thus sung her first and
last, and sung no more.
Farewell, all joys; O Death,
come close mine eyes;
More geese than swans
now live, more fools
than wise.

Today the phrase 'swan song' is still in use to mean a person's final public performance or event.

26   *Tuesday April.* III.

Called on Mr. Foſſik at Magdalen, as arranged, to preſent him with my Records of Dodo's ſong, taking with me my Pipe and Tambour. I was ſurpriſed to find him in Companie with muſical friends. He paid me no reſpect, making tryeing jeſts concerning a dyeing Swan, and a Gibbon, or ſomeſuch, tinkling the while on his Virginals. His foppiſh friends joyned in with their two-pennyworth, a pity the Swan was not a Mute &c. and calling me a Gooſe and a Booby. I went away in diſguſt, and left them to blowing of their own Trumpets.

How tasty was the dodo?

The reviews were mixed:

'…when plucked apparently very good, if tough-skinned.'

'…a little tough even when cooked for a long time.'

'These birds have a stomach great enough to provide two men with a delicious meal; this is the tastiest part of the bird.'

'…they are moderately tasty if tough.' ~~CUT?~~

'The meat of these birds, particularly the breast, is fatty, nourishing, and so plentiful that the meat from three or four has been enough to satisfy a hundred mariners. If they are not cooked till tender or are too old, they are hard to digest.'

'…the longer they were boiled, the tougher and more uneatable they became.' ~~CUT?~~

'…tough and hard, with the exception of the breast and belly, which were very good.'

'…greasy stomachs may seek after them, but to the delicate they are offensive…'

The verdict seems to have been that the dodo was a useful and plentiful source of meat and could be salted away on board for the voyage, but for the discerning there were tastier birds to be had on the island, plus giant tortoises, and sea turtles.

TOO MANY QUOTES.

Wednefday April. IV. ↦ 27

Mr. Sawyer came to fee me. The Bird is plumper, *he faid,* and fit to be ftewed as you would a Goofe, with a ragoo of turnip, carrot, and onion in rich beef gravie; or it might go well in a pie, a Goofe infide of it, and a Fowle infide the Goofe, with butter and forcemeat all around, to be eaten hot or cold, I would not mind. I think he is not ferious in this, defpite his greedy-nefs, and is grown fond of Dodo. The two are alike in plumpneffe and mifchief. He knows well my vow to eat no Meat.

C 2

'He knows well my vow to eat no Meat'

For the Christian, vegetarianism was heretical, a rebellion against the word of God in the Bible. Eating the meat of animals, 'whatever thy soul lusteth after' was one of God's blessings, so long as the confusing proviso 'only ye shall not eat the blood' was overlooked. There were a few dissident voices. John Ray (1627–1705), the naturalist and botanist, pointed out that 'man by nature was never made to be a carnivorous animal, nor is he armed for prey and rapine, with jagged and pointed teeth, but with gentle hands to gather fruit and vegetables, and with teeth to chew and eat them'. John Evelyn, the diarist (1620–1706) in *Acetaria, A Discourse of Sallets* enthused over the healthy wholesomeness of 'the Herby-Diet', while Thomas Tryon (1634–1703) was the most ardent of vegetarians; his numerous publications included *Bill of Fare* which was probably the first vegetarian cookbook in English.

Music

We had a go at playing these sounds on a piano, to get a feel for what the diarist has recorded.

Music type

Music can be typeset by combining individual notes, much like words are typeset from individual letters. Peter de Walpergen is known to have cut over 200 musical notes and symbols for this music type, for use at the University's Press. He probably had only recently finished it, as the earliest appearance noted in the literature is in the Press's type specimen of 1695 (the same year as this diary was printed).

The type specimen calls it 'Musick, Two Line Double Pica', which is the equivalent today of a typesize of about 40 points.

We say much more about the context of these types in **Appendix 9**.

28

Muſic of the Dodo

With the aide of a Reed Pipe and drum, the Dodo's ſounds are here denoted.

1. Sleepeing Song (very quietly, unending)

2. Alarm Call (when disturbed or frightened, a payne to hear)

3. Greetings Call (like a beltch, difgufting)

4. Happinefs Song (with fuggefted words for the beat)

A fplafh of Cream, and

a   crum of Bread

Mr. Sawyer's alternative wording:
A fide of Beef, and a leg of Lamb.

C 3

Mnemonics

Our diarist has added some words to the dodo's Happiness Song. This is an example of a mnemonic, an aid to the memory, from the Greek word *mnēmōn*, meaning mindful.

In this case the invented words are a reminder of the particular rhythm of the bird's song. Here are some birdsong mnemonics the reader may already be familiar with:

'a little bit of bread and no cheese'
—the Yellowhammer

'take two cows Taffy'
—the Wood Pigeon
(a slur on the Welsh for their supposed weakness for cattle thieving)

'my toe bleeds, Betty'
—the Chiffchaff

'teacher, teacher'
—the Great Tit

'wet my lips'
—the Quail

Driving many people mad during the summer months is the monotonous song of the Collared Dove. To football enthusiasts it sounds like 'United, United'.

Bicycles

Although we said that we would not comment on the dreams mentioned in the diary, there is often an exception to every rule. It sounds like Mr Flay is dreaming of a bicycle of some kind.

In Medieval times there were wooden horses on four wheels, pulled along by helpers, the man astride tilting his lance at a quintain, a target on a post. One such is shown in the margin of a fourteenth-century illuminated manuscript in the Bodleian Library, Oxford.

Wooden horses on wheels for a child to sit on were in use in the sixteenth century, some pulled or pushed, others apparently propelled by the rider's feet. A book by Edward Somerset, *A Century of the Names and Scantlings and Inventions by me already practised* of 1655 describes 'an artificial horse ... fit for running at the Ring, on

---

30   *Thurſday April.* v.

Mr. Tompkyns in viſiting today was taken with a ſtrange ſwooning Melancholie, and was too feeble to return to his Lodgings, wherever they might be. I have let him lie in my bed till he has regained his ſtrength. Meanwhile I muſt ſleepe on the floor. I had hoped the Draweings might be ready for Mr. Aſhmole's coming to Oxford in May to open his Muſæum.

A new Dreame of Mr. Flay's. I ſaw machines, *he ſaid*, ſomething like Hobby-Horſes, a wheel before and behind, and a man ſeated between ſomehow, moving his legs as if he were running in air, and making no tread upon the Ground; nevertheleſs the wheels turned

---

which a man being mounted, with his lance in his hand, he can at pleasure make him start, and swiftly to run his career, using the decent posture with bon grace ... and running as swiftly as if he rode upon a Barbe' (that is a Barbary horse from the north coast of Africa).

There is also a tantalizing brief note by the diarist John Evelyn of John Wilkins (see the note besides the 2 April diary entry) with Robert Hooke, and William Petty, experimenting with 'contrivances for chariots' and 'a wheel on which to run races'.

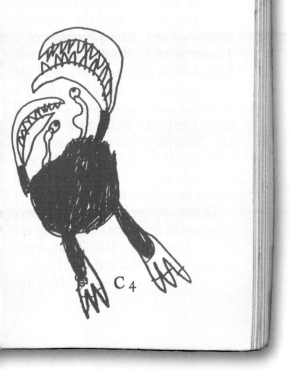

turned to move the machine foreward. There was a hoſt of theſe
Conveyances, travelling at ſpeed,
ſingly or in pairs.

C 4

Another child's drawing.
Perhaps it is a crab? It seems
to be in the same style as
the drawing on the diary
page for 1 April, but a bit
more detailed—perhaps
the child is older by now?

Mr. T. Buglass,
New Denham,
Middleton,
MDPOR.

Between these two pages
of the diary was found an
envelope, addressed to a
Mr T. Buglass, concerning
a sheepdog. The contents
are shown overleaf.

DIRECTORS:
D.OLIVER (Chairman)
S.B.OLIVER.
J.K.M OLIVER (Managing)
R.RIDDELL.
W.D.E.INCH.

ALL COMMUNICATIONS TO BE
ADDRESSED TO THE COMPANY.

TELEGRAMS:
OLIVERS, AUCTIONEERS, HAWICK.
TELEPHONES:
HAWICK 2126 & 3152 (2 LINES)

ANDREW OLIVER & SON, LIMITED.

AUCTIONEERS, LIVE STOCK AGENTS, VALUATORS & ESTATE AGENTS.

Auction Mart,

HAWICK 4th April, 1956.

Dear Mr. Buglass,

I got your letter about a dog and will do my best to try and get you a suitable one. They are not very easily picked up at the moment but will keep a lookout, and will communicate with you again should a likely one turn up. With kind regards.

Yours faithfully,

[signature]

Per. *Pass Train.*

[handwritten] Mr R Buglass
New Deanham
Chollerton Station
via Reedsmouth, Redesmouth

From A. Oliver & Son, Ltd.,
AUCTIONEERS, HAWICK.

Above
is the label that was
tied around the sheepdog,
named Hemp, on his 50-mile train
journey across the Scottish border to
Northumberland in England. On the reverse
of the label is a receipt showing that it cost 6s. 9d.
to send this 'parcel'. The single track Border Counties
Railway closed to passengers just four months later.

ALL COMMUNICATIONS TO BE
ADDRESSED TO THE COMPANY.

ANDREW OLIVER & SON, LIMITED.

AUCTIONEERS, LIVE STOCK AGENTS, VALUATORS & ESTATE AGENTS.

TELEGRAMS:
OLIVERS, AUCTIONEERS, HAWICK.
TELEPHONE.
Nº 2126 HAWICK.

Auction Mart,

HAWICK

2nd June, 1956.

Dear Mr. Buglass,

Thanks for your letter, the dog will be put
on the afternoon train on Tuesday addressed to Chollerton
Station and will get there about 6.24. and I have no
doubt you will receive him all right.

The dog's name is "HEMP" and Mr. Burns who
has had charge of him for some time says that you should
keep him on a chain at night until he gets used to his
new surroundings. He runs by both voice and whistle.

To get him to run left call "Come bye".

To get him to run right call "quay to me".
This is a Scotch expression
for "Come away to me"

Whistle to stop.

The dog looks a good price but they are hardly
to be got just now, especially a good one. I feel sure
you will be highly pleased with this one, he is a nice
dog to look at, has a nice nature, and a very strong runner
and afraid of nothing.

Yours sincerely,

[signature]

COME BYE

Sheep

QUAY TO ME

Left hand   Right hand

Whistle to stop.

ANDREW OLIVER & SON, LTD.,
Auctioneers, Hawick,

26th June . 1956.

Dear Mr. Buglass,

Got the dog back all right and very
sorry he did so badly for you. He is
working all right here but has to be firmly
handled. I think part of his trouble is
that he has had too little to do and is too
fresh. Better luck some other time maybe.

Yours sincerely,

[signature]

. and the unsuccessful ending to this tale.

Flightless birds
There are forty species of flightless birds still in existence today. They are believed to have evolved from flying ancestors because of the evidence of their vestigial wings. But it is possible that some may be descended from creatures that never had that ability. There is much convincing anatomical evidence to suggest a line of descent from dinosaurs to birds. The moas of New Zealand, all extinct since the seventeenth century, were very large flightless birds with egg-shaped bodies, sturdy legs, and tiny heads, and had no vestiges of wings at all. A New Zealand song bemoans their loss:

> Can't get 'em,
> They've et 'em,
> They're gone and there
> ain't no moa!

Most flightless birds are, or were, found on islands, like the dodo on Mauritius, where there were no four-legged mammals to compete with. New Zealand had more flightless birds than any other. Until a thousand years ago it had no mammals other than bats. An exception to the island preference is the ostrich, which has survived on the African savannah, using speed and sharp claws to defend itself.

---

32   *Friday April.* VI. ♉

Dodo grows but its wings are mere ſtumps, unlikely to ſupport ſuch a bulk in Flight. To teſt this I had the aſſiſtance of Mr. Sawyer and Mr. Flay in climbing with the Bird into the topmoſt rafters of my Attic, by way of a Tower of table, ſtooles, and boxes, from which eminence Mr. Sawyer prepared to let fall Dodo, to ſee if it would at leaſt flap its Wings. I had taken the precaution of perſuading Mr. Tompkyns to come out of his bed, which he did reluctantly, and to pile it up with clokes, bedding &c. to ſave chance of injurie.

Dodo dropp'd like a ſtone, rebounded from the bed with great force, knocking Mr. Tompkyns downe where he ſtood watching.

                   Neither

Friday April. VI. ♓ 33

Neither ſuffered great hurt, except in dignitie. *Demonſtratio:* Dodo lacks natural proclivitie for Flight.

So did no Dodo ever poſſeſs ſuch power? How then did it get to its Iſland? By walking there from the door of the Ark on Ararat? By bridges of Land ſince waſhed away? It is a race of Bird grown fat and lazy, *ſaid Mr. Sawyer.* I told him that all creatures are as God made them at the Creation, they have not changed. I have dreamed often of flying, *ſaid Mr. Flay.*

The Ark

Athanasius Kircher (1602–1680), a German Jesuit scholar devoted to arcane learning, was not unusual for his time in believing that science would support Christian doctrine by showing that the Bible was literally true. He speculated on the dimensions of the Ark given in Genesis, the three storeys of accommodation, the number of species on board, the logistics of feeding (extra animals for the carnivores?), disposal of dung, etc.

His book *Arca Noë* of 1675 illustrates the Ark as a large rectangular box-like craft and includes detailed plans for each deck. But it was not long before travellers began to return to Europe with accounts or actual specimens of previously unknown creatures, and the number to be accommodated on board the Ark swelled at a disturbing rate. By the nineteenth century, a literal interpretation of the story in Genesis was treated by most scientists as implausible.

Mount Ararat is the site in modern-day Turkey where the Ark is supposed to have beached itself at the retreating of the Flood.

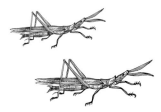

34 *Saturday April.* VII.

At my prompting, Mr. Tomp-kyns ſuffered himſelf to be propp'd up in bed ſo that he might continue with his Draweings, but he was a picture of Lethargiqueneſſe, and ſoon enough ſank back. The Bird is greater than when I laſt looked at it, *he ſaid*.

What is the matter with Mr. Tompkyns? He eats nothing and takes but a little Hippocraſs to cleanſe the bloode and ſharpen the brain. Mr. Sawyer is gone out to diſcover if anyone knows the poor man. That he is from London and is a Painter is all we know. He made my acquaintance at the Coffee-Houſe, as if he knew me.

Hippocrass
This is a wine which is flavoured with spices and strained through a conical bag called a 'Hippocrates' sleeve' (after the ancient Greek physician).

This black and white photograph found between these pages is probably from the 1950s or 1960s and shows a Jack Russell Terrier in front of a snowy garden. On the reverse of the photographic paper is printed the words 'Kodak Velox paper F140'. We wonder why this photograph would be here. Is there any link to the dog 'Hemp' a few pages back?

Sunday April. VIII. ○   35

My Landlord viſited to ſee Mr. Tompkyns, if he is a danger to the Houſe, quite ignoring Dodo, which he had not ſeen before now, but knew of, by report. The ſerving-girl Mary will come when her work allows, to care for the ſick man. The mid-wife, Mrs. Spott, who lives below us, and is known for match-making, bone-ſetting, love potions, and finding loſt things, told us to trye freſh killed Pigeons to the ſoles of Mr. Tompkyns' feet. Ignorant ſuperſtition, burn the Witch, *ſaid Mr. Sawyer*, but ſhe is quite deaf and took no notice.

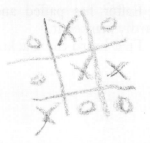

Mrs Spott
Mrs Spott is a wisewoman, or cunning woman, a reassuring figure to those unable to afford a physician or unwilling to consult a stranger. Their traditional herbal remedies, spells, and experience of a wide range of situations usually did more good than harm, though they were vulnerable to accusations of being in league with the devil and were roundly condemned by men of science, the medical profession, and the church.

Pigeons do seem to have had a connection in folklore with death and illness. If a pigeon alighted on a bed or house, someone was likely to suffer. Pigeons were frequently used in cures—for instance, a live bird might be cut in half and applied to the patient's body to draw out fever. The famous seventeenth-century diarist Samuel Pepys twice mentions this remedy.

Noughts and crosses
An inconclusive game of noughts and crosses in brilliant green wax crayon. The game (known in the United States of America as Tic-Tac-Toe) is a simplified version of the ancient Nine Man's Morris or Merels, originally played with a board and counters. A similar pattern has been found engraved in the stonework of the Temple of Kurna in Egypt, built around 1440 BC.

The Cuckoo (*Cuckulus canorus***)**

The sound of this secretive spring visitor has made a great impression on English people, from the thirteenth-century monk who wrote the famous song with the opening lines 'Sumer is icumen in, Lhude sing cuccu' (which translates as 'Summer is coming in, loudly sings the cuckoo'), to the correspondents of the letters pages of *The Times* of London, who compete each year to record the earliest hearing.

It would be interesting to know where our diarist was at the time he heard the cuckoo. Folklore suggests he would be lucky if he heard it to his right, unlucky to his left, or behind him; if he was in bed he would suffer illness, unless he got up and started running at once; and if he was standing on earth or stone he would be dead before the next Spring.

Our diarist's first cuckoo comes quite early on in the year. The earliest in recent times was 20 February 1953 at Farnham in Surrey. The cuckoo is however rarely heard these days; its numbers are falling. You are even less likely to hear the call of the female cuckoo, once described as 'rather like the sudden rush of water through a narrow-necked bottle'. We are fond of the cuckoo's song, but not of its parasitic reproductive habits in leaving its eggs in other birds' nests. For a long time people believed that the young cuckoo bit off the head of its foster mother. The cuckoo has also been associated with adultery— a betrayed husband is known as a *cuckold*.

---

36   *Monday April.* ix. ♉

Mr. Tompkyns is no better and nothing can be difcovered of his Lodgings or his Companie before he became our gueft. Now he will not fpeak or raife himfelf out of bed. Dodo fits upon him for warmth. My Experiments have ftopp'd; inftead I trye my hand at Draweing the Bird whenever it is ftill. Mrs. Spott comes to fee the Patient, to prefs foul drenches downe his throat and examine his bodilye excretions. When her duties are done Mary comes to fit with him; it feems to comfort him.

Eafter has paffed and I have hardly marked it.

Firft heard the Cuckow.

Tuefday April. x.   37

Took downe my Mirror to difcover if Dodo will recognife itfelf therin. It fhewed no intereſt in the Mirror, but as fomething it liked to get behind. Alas it fmafhed the Glafs with one blow of its dreadful Beak. This brings more than bad luck, it was a Gift of my Father to me on my coming up to Oxford; the ornate frame is cracked too.

Dodo has batter'd a hole through the Wall to reach the Pigeons and Fowles in the next-door Room. It would not ſtopp and was ſtuck halfway. Mr. Sawyer made the hole greater yet by his efforts to free the Bird. He will mifs my Mirror greatly for the appraifal of his foppifh new Clothes.

Mirrors
Breaking mirrors has long been associated with bad luck. The earliest printed reference we could find to this belief was from 1777, so this reference in the diary appears to predate that.

The idea of seven years of bad luck arrived in the mid-nineteenth century. Why seven years? This may derive from a Roman belief that man was physically rejuvenated every seven years.

Many other superstitions have accumulated around mirrors. A baby who is allowed to look into one will get rickets or become cross-eyed. A woman can see her intended spouse in a mirror if she sits in front of it, eats an apple and brushes her hair; alternatively she should walk backwards downstairs looking into a mirror. Mirrors should be covered if there has been a death in the house, while you sleep, and if there are thunderstorms about. The diarist should have thought of Mr Tompkyns, as mirrors should also be covered in a sickroom.

Pigeons
This illustration is labelled *Columba Anglica* in a book by the sixteenth century Swiss naturalist Conrad Gesner. Its feathered feet and crest are similar to some modern varieties. Men have been breeding pigeons for variety of body and feather shape, colour, markings, and speed since ancient times. All pigeons are descended from a single species, the Rock pigeon (*Columba livia*). Charles Darwin made a close study of the selective breeding of pigeons and the opening pages of his *Origin of Species* are devoted to them. Remember, the dodo is a kind of pigeon. More on pigeons to come.

38   *Wednefday April.* XI. ♓

My Landlord's Pigeons and Fowles began to come through the hole into my Room, and Dodo to go t'other way, fo we have put my Cheft acrofs to barr the way. My Landlord was not vexed; he propofes vifits of my Bird to his for good Society. It will be an Experiment to fee how it goes, for both Men and Beafts profper by good Companie, fruitful difpute, goffipping &c. On Mauritius Dodos muft needs mix with all forts of creatures; it cannot be good for my Bird to be among Men only for fo long.

Dodo eats my rufh Mat.

Thur∫day April. XII.   39

Ra∫cally children's faces ∫hew
at the Window of the Hou∫e
acro∫s the Alley, tryeing to ∫ee my
Bird, ∫houting and throwing crums
of bread, or nuts, or grain. I mu∫t
leave open my Window in ca∫e they
break the Gla∫s, and Dodo ha∫tens
to get their Gifts.

Took Dodo in to the Fowles
and Pigeons. They were wary, but
Dodo lords it among∫t them and
would eat all their feed in a minute,
if I let it. Mr. Sawyer came hot
from the Tennis Court after a poor
game, he ∫aid, and ∫tayed a while
to watch Dodo and his new found
friends.

Real Tennis
This must be referring
to Real Tennis, which is
the forerunner of today's
Lawn Tennis. It is played
indoors and shares the
same scoring system. It can
be played by two or four
people. Service is always
delivered from the same
side of the court, into the
'hazard' side. A small solid
ball is hit with rackets over
the net, or off the side walls.
Its origins can be traced to a
game played in monastery
cloisters in the eleventh
century, initially with a bare
or gloved hand. There are
a handful of Real Tennis
courts still in use today
including one at Merton
College, Oxford, where a
polite request may enable
you to watch a game.

POSITION
OKAY?
↓

More
el

Noughts and crosses
Apparently there are 255,168 possible games of
Noughts and Crosses. The first computer program
designed to play the game was written in 1952 by
A. S. Douglas as part of his PhD dissertation on
Human–Computer Interaction. The computer was
the EDSAC machine, the first true programmable
computer, built at Cambridge University in 1949.

42

A bookmark found in the diary:

This bookmark was issued by the Ministry of Health, but presumably written by the COI, or Central Office of Information, which was founded in 1946.

The COI works on public information campaigns for various British government and public sector bodies. In its early years a Dr Richard Massingham explained how to blow your nose to avoid spreading germs. In later campaigns Dave Prowse starred in the Green Cross Code advertisements on road safety (he later become Darth Vader in the original Star Wars films), and Olympic medal winner David Wilkie helped those who wanted to learn to swim.

Crown Copyright * 1964

... and the other side of the bookmark

DANGER

The more cigarettes you smoke, the greater the risk of death from lung cancer, chronic bronchitis, or heart disease

YOU HAVE BEEN WARNED

Issued by the Ministry of Health

Printed for H.M. Stationery Office by M.M.P. Ltd. P10691-8/64-$772

With a delightful sense of wit, the owner of this bookmark has scribbled their unhealthy shopping list on the other side:

> ¼ Bottle Dimple Haig
>
> ¼ Bottle Johnny Walker
>
> 20 Rothmans cork tip [?] or Embassy

'The Dimple' or 'Pinch' is a blended Scotch Whisky, first produced in 1888 by John Aloysius Haig, who was from a well-established whisky-making family. Indeed, the earliest documented reference to a distillery company still operating today concerns one Robert Haig being summoned before the Church elders in 1655 for operating a still on the Sabbath (Sunday). The name 'Pinch' is used in the United States, where the distinctive shape of bottle was the first example of its class to be patented in 1958. Haig Scotch Whisky often advertised itself with the slogan 'Don't be vague. Ask for Haig'.

Johnny Walker whisky dates back to 1820 when one John Walker opened a shop in Kilmarnock and quickly gained a reputation for this fine blend of Scotch whisky.

A still for distilling alcohol

And why would someone draw a millimetre scale on a bookmark?

At night I ſtill have my Brazier for its warmth and light, and to bake a Potato or two. My friends were gathered here to hear Mr. Flay's new Dreame, told to the muſic of my pipe; Mr. Sawyer ſmokes and drinks ale, Dodo ſleepes beſide Mary, and Mr. Tompkyns ſeems to be attentive.

In my dreame I was walking on a ſtreet, *ſaid Mr. Flay*, and looking downe ſaw my boots and ſhadow over two yellow Lines running as far as the eye could ſee. The centre of the ſtreet was divided into halves, this time by a daſh'd white Line juſt like a running ſtitch, but on a gigantic ſcale. Elſewhere there were braſs markers over Tombs, figured with crude patterns and names.

names. I recall Ductile Stanton,
Earth Rod, Integral Slideout;
some family tombs, such as Dean &
Sons, though quite small, as if they
were interr'd upright or reduced
somehow to save space; sometimes
an open Grille with trash and
water below and sometimes small
Windows of thick Glass. On the
Paving, were dry leaves and spots
of white and black, a little raised
and smooth-edged, like something
press'd downe. That is all. It is a
pity you could not raise your head
to see more, *said Mr. Sawyer.* What
kind of boots did you wear?

D

Quite what a 1973 receipt for 84 pence worth of sole fish, bought from a High Class Fishmongers in the north of England, is doing in the diary is a question the editors would like to be able to answer.

PHONE: NEWCASTLE 811440

81 HOLLY AVENUE.   3 ACORN ROAD,
JESMOND.   JESMOND.

NEWCASTLE-UPON-TYNE. 2

Nov 8. 1967

M

Bought of

SIMPSON'S
HIGH CLASS FISHMONGERS

Sole   .84

46

How ſhall I call Dodo, ſtill igno-rant if it be a he or a ſhe? No-one has the courage to determine the ſex now it is ſo big. I will call it Him. To Mr. Sawyer it is her Majeſtie the Queen. To Mr. Flay it is nothing in particular, merely Dodo; and to Mary it is Diddums. To Mr. Tompkyns it is alas no more than a kind of Paper-Weight that holds him downe, not that he minds it or anything come to that. He is no better.

Mr. Sawyer brought me anoth-er Frog in his pocket to ſee Dodo eat it. The creature made ſuch valient leaps to eſcape that I caught it up and later gave it lib-erty.

A frog.

Sunday April. xv. 43

Mr. Sawyer went yefterday to the Apothecary to enquire on behalf of poor Mr. Tompkyns. Returning, he faid he had fuffered a lecture on the Humours, and was given a coftly Preparation of Herbs to put into a Bath for the Patient, then we fhould wrap him in Sheepfkins for a day and a night to fweat out inward corruptions, give him a reftorative of three pints of new milk, one of red wine, twenty four yolks of new-layed eggs, fine white bread all beaten together, then we muft put Horfe Dung on the Coals and drawe the fumes into his clothes, and give him fpirit of fal amoniac. Mary and Mrs. Spott will undertake this.

D 2

Apothecary

The apothecary was something like a combination of the present-day chemist and a GP. From his shop he diagnosed illnesses and prescribed his home-made preparations. Most of these were based on herbs, alongside some wonder drugs from abroad (opium and rhubarb), and some occult ingredients (spiders' webs and moss from human skulls). Increasingly these were replaced by ready-made products such as Daffy's Elixir and Simpson's Golden Eye Ointment, that would still be available in the twentieth century. Like the wisewoman, the apothecary was resorted to by those unable to pay the physician's hefty fees, and business boomed.

Humours

The Humours were the bodily fluids associated with illness since Hippocrates, the fifth-century Greek physician. They were blood, yellow bile (choler), black bile (melancholy), and phlegm. The main purpose of medicine was to maintain an equilibrium between these humours. This could be done either by diet or draining surplus by bleeding, blistering, laxatives, or enemas.

44 *Monday April.* XVI. ● ☿

An Experiment was tried to difcover if Dodo recognizes us as particular bodies, as I believe he does, and if it is by our faces, our form, our manner of movement, or our clothes. He runs always to me as I am the one to feed him (and he is ever hungry). I came into the room with my face entirely hid by a fcarf, and he knew me. I put on the clothes of Mr. Tompkyns, entered agayne, and he knew me. I wrapped myfelf in Mr. Sawyer's cloake, wore his hat and cutt up Mr. Tompkyns' brufhes for a beard, and he knew me agayne. When I put on a Bear Coftume Mr. Sawyer had once for a mafque, and came in roaring, it gave him paufe a while, but then he knew me. Mr. Sawyer entered in my

Sitting between these pages was a metal tag dated 1855, with the name 'George Hogg'. It might have been a furniture maker's mark that was nailed to the piece after it had been made, but the editors are not quite sure.

Monday April. XVI. ● ♉ 45

my clothes, the few he could make fit, and was ignored. Then Mr. Sawyer got from Mrs. Spott fome of her clothes (he can charm anyone if he fo wifhes) and I wore them with a wigg of ftrawe and a falfe nofe of dough. This caufed Dodo to retreat into a dark corner. Mrs. Spott would not put on mine or Mr. Sawyer's clothing, and Mary call'd us cruel to torment the Bird fo. The cafe for Recognition or no is not proved, *faid Mr. Flay,* the Bird has run away from fear of Man's Madnefs.

D 3

Recognition

If the diarist was suddenly presented with a roomful of dodos of the same age, he would undoubtedly be hard pressed to recognize his own bird amongst them. But birds are good at recognizing individuals of their own kind, particularly kin, and also seem able to recognize human individuals, both those they have been raised by or become used to. Perhaps the madness in the friends' conduct during the experiment was because of the influence of the full moon.

The earlier experiment with the mirror might have led to the deduction that birds are more likely to attack their reflection, believing it to be a rival stranger, than recognize it as themselves. The mirror test of self-awareness, used by scientists today, sees what reaction a creature makes after a mark is surreptitiously put on its head and it is then shown its reflection. If it puts its hand up to the mark this is believed to be evidence of self-awareness. The test has only been passed conclusively so far by humans (over the age of eighteen months) and apes.

50

The academic year
At this time there were four
terms in the University's
academic year: Michaelmas,
Hilary, Easter, and Trinity.
Since 1918 there are three:
Michaelmas (1 October
to 17 December), Hilary
(7 January to 25 March or
the Sunday before Palm
Sunday, whichever is
earlier), and Trinity (20 April
or the Wednesday after
Easter, whichever is later,
to 6 July).
    Saint Hilary was a
fourth-century Bishop
of Poitiers, whose feast
day is 13 January. Saint
Michael the Archangel's
feast day, Michaelmas, is
29 September.

A parcel of Food and Bookes
comes from my Father, with a
Letter to tell me his health recov-
ers, and what is leſs welcome to hear,
he intends to viſit me in Oxford
when his ſtrength is ſufficient for
the Journey. Can I once more aſk
of Mr. Sawyer that he play the part
of the great Surgeon I am ſuppos'd
to be apprenticed to, and ſinge my
praiſes and the magnificence of my
proſpects, all the while on a rack
of tenterhookes left our decep-
tion be diſcovered? And will my
conſcience let me go on with ſuch
folly? Perhaps your Father's health
will not improve, *ſaid Mr. Sawyer*.
Term begins tomorrow and I muſt
keep my friends away : they are too
much diſtracted from their ſtudies.

Wednefday April. xviii.   47

Now Dodo batters at the door of my Prefs to get to the hole in the wall and be with his friends the Fowles and Pigeons. He is a Machine of Deftruction. When he wearies of this he likes to hang by his Beak from the table top and fwing himfelf, or chafe a Skittle Ball. But then it is ftrange how he leaves off thefe Frolicks to ftand facing a piece of wall for an age as if in a trance, and will not be diftracted by any means. The moft of Dodo's time is fpent in afking to eat, following me, and entreating me with clappings of his Beak.

D 4

Beaks

A bird's beak is shaped according to what it eats. There are beaks for cracking, shredding, spearing, chiselling, probing, shovelling, hoovering, levering, and straining. Most are designed to do other things too, such as grooming or fighting. The toucan illustrated above may use its exceptionally large and colourful beak to attract a mate, intimidate other birds, or reach distant food. Some beaks seem as multi-purpose as a Swiss army knife.

Beaks are a bony elongation of the skull, covered in a layer of keratin, the same material as our fingernails, surprisingly light considering its strength. The pigeon (we keep coming back to them) has magnetite in its beak, an iron-rich crystal with magnetic properties, allowing it to navigate using the earth's magnetic field.

Scientists, by the way, prefer to call them bills.

Play

The dodo's behaviour seems extraordinary, but crows and sparrows have been seen sliding on snow, and toucans tossing fruit to each other. Is this play?

The Museum
The Old Ashmolean Museum, now the Museum of the History of Science, stands in Broad Street, between the Sheldonian Theatre and Exeter College (see the maps in **Appendix 10**). The tidying of the site referred to by the diarist is in preparation for the grand opening on 21 May. Work on the building had begun in 1679 when the University accepted Elias Ashmole's gift of the famous Tradescant Collection of Rarities, agreeing to his condition that a suitable building be erected to house it. The cost of the Museum was a ruinous £4,530.

Suspicions
The diarist's sniffy suggestion that Ashmole 'did not get the collection himself' reminds us that it was the Tradescants, father and son, who had amassed the collection, and of the suspicious circumstances under which it came to Ashmole. John Tradescant the Younger, who died in 1662, had apparently made a gift of it to Ashmole three years earlier, but his will made no mention of this. Perhaps he had changed his mind. Ashmole won the subsequent legal case to uphold his claim, subjecting Tradescant's widow to what appeared to be harassment until she had handed it all over.

On the other hand, this suspicion is perhaps unfair to Ashmole. He did

contribute books, coins, and medals from his own collection, and it was his energy, persistence, and ambition that led to a building that was the country's first institutional museum open to the public (seventy years before the British Museum), the first specifically designed for the study of science, and the first purpose-built chemical laboratory.

48   *Thurſday April*. xix. Ⅱ

Got ſome work clearing the land about the new Muſæum and was able to go inſide to ſee Mr. Aſhmole's Colleċtion as it begins to be inſtalled.

A great jumble of rubbiſhy dead and duſty ſtuff we are ſuppoſed to admire, rarities claiming a place by being merely Freekiſh, ſuch as a hundred faces carved on a cherry-ſtone. He did not even get the Colleċtion himſelf but puts his name to it. Among a crowd of Birds and bits of Birds on a ſhelf was his Dodo I ſaw before, fat and ugly as I truſt mine will never be. How different this diſmall thing was in compariſon to my beautiful living Bird. I could not breathe and came away. I was not ſuppoſed to

Thurſday April. xix. ♊ 49

to be there and was rebuked for it.

Maſons were ſtill at work carv-
ing ſhells, grapes and ſuchlike on
the outſide. Mr. Wood was ſhew-
ing ſome Viſitors his Building,
one of them a little fellow I heard
addreſſed as Mr. Wren, who was
once a prodigy here at Oxford,
but is now in London to purſue his
Architecture. He was one of thoſe
Great Men I came here to emulate,
in vain alas. I looked on him with
intereſt and wiſhed to liſten to his
converſation but my workmen's
clothes made me unfit to be in his
Companie. With him was another
man, called Hawk, I think.

A third game of noughts and crosses. Unlike
the previous two, this one is in purple crayon.

Hawk

Could the 'Hawk' mentioned in the diary entry above be
another great English architect, Nicholas Hawksmoor
(1661–1736), later to design the Clarendon Building and parts
of All Souls College, both only yards from this site? At this
time Hawksmoor was twenty two years old, serving his
apprenticeship as 'scholar and domestic clerk' with Wren.

If you stand between
the Museum and the
Sheldonian Theatre, and
look above the Museum's
grand doorway, you will
see the tall carved panels
of marine life flanking the
central window.

Mr Wood

Mr Wood is undoubtedly
Thomas Wood, the
probable designer of the
Museum, known to be
an Oxford Master Mason.
For someone whose only
other known design is
the tower of a church at
Deddington in Oxfordshire,
it's an impressive piece
of work, particularly this
great ceremonial doorway,
apparently never used.

Mr Wren

Mr Wren is surely
Christopher Wren
(1632–1723), England's
greatest architect, who
came to Wadham College
as an undergraduate in
1650 and quickly acquired
the reputation of a brilliant
designer of experimental
models, tackling everything
from glass beehives, a
mechanical weather
recorder, submarines, and
speaking statues. He was
Professor of Astronomy by
the age of twenty eight.

He then turned his
energies to architecture.
His first major building was
the Sheldonian Theatre,
completed in 1669. He was
drawn away from Oxford
by his greatest challenges:
St Paul's Cathedral, the
city of London churches,
Greenwich, and Hampton
Court. He was probably
visiting the site to see how
the Museum sat alongside
his own Theatre and to
assess a building that may
have been inspired by his
own earlier designs for a
similar project in London
that had come to nothing.

50   *Friday April.* xx.

What elſe did you ſee at the Muſæum? *aſked Mr. Sawyer.* I have heard tell of Tammahacks, poyſoned arrows, and bloode that rayned downe in the Iſle of Wight. What of the flea chain, three hundred links in yet an inch? *enquired Mr. Flay.* I rebuked my friends. Why was Freekiſh ſtuff more worthy of diſplay than ſuch a marvel of livelineſs as my Dodo, or indeed one of my Landlord's Pigeons? But they were not perſuaded; the reputation of the Rarities is ſo great, and when it is opened to the Public's view they will be firſt at the Door.

WRONG PERIOD!

Saturday *April.* XXI. ♋ 51

I was awake in the night and saw as if in a Dreame Mr. Tompkyns wrapt in a Blanket, standing at the Window in the light of the Moon. I did not speak out but must have fallen back to sleepe, for I remember no more. In the morning Mr. Tompkyns lay in the bed as we have become accustomed to seeing him. This was forgot (till I write it now) in the displays of rage and weeping today from Mr. Flay when he came to us, to inform us that his Tutor called him a bone-brained idle wretch. You must challenge him to a Duel, *said Mr. Sawyer.*

+ LOOKS AMERICAN ↓

Duels

There was a vogue for duelling at this time, especially among the upper classes and members of the court. King Charles II attempted to stamp it out by law.

University law was set out in the statutes known as the Laudian Code of 1636, commissioned by the Chancellor William Laud, also Archbishop of Canterbury. Among the many things forbidden to students were dice, cards, rope-dancing, ball-play, hunting wild animals, idling, wandering, loitering, going into wine shops, smoking, long hair, frequenting harlots, sword matches, the carrying of arms, and dibs. Laud was beheaded in 1645 following a charge of high treason, but his Code continued to be the basis of University law until 1854. Dibs, by the way, seems to have been a game played with small stones, otherwise known as dabs or dabstones.

Duelling would have resulted in immediate expulsion.

56

An artist's palette.

I muſt Drawe Dodo now that Mr.
Tompkyns will not do it, but
my ſkill in Draweing is ſmall. My
friends trye their hand, but it is
hopeleſs. Mr. Sawyer holds downe
her Majeſtie by main force to copy
her outline, then drew her ſhadow
in a candle-flame, ſingeing her
feathers. A child could do better,
ſaid Mr. Flay. Dodo walks through
our colours ſo at the leaſt I have
ſome foote-prints. We leave off and
go onto the roof to lie on the tiles
to ſinge nonſenſe Songs. Both my
friends do no work for their ſtudies
and contrive always to avoid it; it
ſeems I am the only one to have
a Purpoſe, my Experiments, of
which they ſeem jealous.

Monday April. XXIII. ☉ ♌ 53

We have been upon the roof agayne, it has been fo warm, and from our vantage we look upon the Spire of St. Mary the Virgin, the octagon Cupola of Sheldon's Theatre, and that fancifull new embellifhement of Mr. Wren's, Chrift Church Tower. Below is the open window of Mrs. Spott's room, and we fee her without her wigg, peering into her Venus Glaffe. Mr. Sawyer makes paper Birds of his miferable fketches to throw at her and then hides himfelf behind a Chimney. Later he came back filthee drunk wearing red Flowers of ribbon and wept over Mr. Tomkyns.

The rooftop view

St Mary the Virgin is the parish church of Oxford in the High Street, looking much the same today as it did in the diarist's time. The newest addition was the remarkable porch of 1637 with its barley sugar columns. Sheldon's Theatre is the Sheldonian Theatre, and Mr Wren's 'fancifull' new tower is Tom Tower at Christ Church, completed in 1682 (see Oxford maps in **Appendix 10**).

Venus Glass

This seems to have been something like a crystal ball, containing egg-white suspended in water, in which the fortune teller could see shapes and figures.

St George's Day

The dragon-slaying St George was widely celebrated with feasts and processions on 23 April all through the middle ages, but then interest faded or was discouraged. The custom of wearing the traditional red rose of England is rarely seen today. Enthusiasm for St George's flag (a red cross on a white ground) has been revived by English football fans since the European Cup Finals of 1996 and the World Cup of 1998.

A spider illustrated

This torn page fragment was found alongside the diary reference to spiders. It looks like a copper engraving from the nineteenth century.

The caption to the spider has been torn out separately and glued underneath it. The caption reads 'Lycosa *sabulosa. Hahn.*' which is its Latin name, followed by the author who classified it, Hahn. After a bit of research, the classification was found to date to 1831, but this has since been superseded, and its Latin name is now Lycosidae *Alopecosa cursor.*

There's a vertical line above the engraving of the spider and this is probably its actual size. Since we've had to reduce the engraving, we should say that it actually measures 15mm long. Some Wolf spiders can be as large as 80mm long.

54   *Tuesday April.* xxiv.

Eager to get spiders from holes in my walls, Dodo will use his Beak or Claw with dexteritie. If this fails, he will take up a knife in his Beak, to poke them out. My Friends do not believe me, but I saw it. Mr. Sawyer offers the Bird, in jest, a pen to write, a combe, scissors, a loaf to cutt, &c.

Without hands a Bird must use its Beak always. To observe how a man might fare I bound the arms of my Friends to their bodyes, and set them certayne tasks. But they would not be serious, falling downe, laughing, cock-a-doodle-doing. So I put a stopp to it, learning nothing. Mr. Tompkyns was in terror at their horseplay, and Dodo hid himself.

Animal Kingdom

1. Lycosa *sabulosa. Hahn.* 2. Lycosa *cur*

Wednesday April. xxv. ♍ 55

I have said no more of Mr. Tompkyns for this reason: there is nothing to tell; he lies mute and feeble, taking sips of gruel and morsels of bread from Mary. She attends him with great compaſſion, waſhes and ſhaves him, sings ſongs to comfort him &c. It is ſtrange that not one jot of information has come of our enquiries regarding his Life before he appeared among us.

A Dreame of my own laſt night. I ſtood upon an iſland and all over was covered in little Birds, which perched upon my arms and feet and head, quite tame. Nearby were Flamingoes, Pelikans, and other ſtrange Birds, walking unafraid.

Time on their hands
Filling in letters has been with us for a long time, and it looks like someone has relatively recently practised their skills here. At least it is still pretty clear what the entry says. It has been done in blue felt-tip pen.

Tamatia

We've put this bird in because we like it. It's from a book by the seventeenth-century engraver Matthäus Merian and is labelled Tamatia. Perhaps it's the spotted Puffbird (Bucco tamatia) of South America, hard to spot because it spends a lot of time motionless.

Do horses count?

Mr Sawyer may well have seen such an act. The most famous was William Banks with his horse Marocco, in Elizabethan times. As well as counting figures on dice, picking cards, retrieving, dancing, and playing dead, Marocco reputedly climbed the spiral steps to the top of St Paul's Cathedral in London.

A German horse called Clever Hans could add, subtract, multiply, divide, work with fractions, tell the time, read, and spell. He was investigated in 1904 by a panel of eminent scientists. Psychologist Oskar Pfungst determined that the horse was not really performing these tasks, but responding to tiny signals in the body language and facial expressions of his trainer, who was apparently unaware of what he was doing. These signals and a visible release of tension showed the horse when it had reached the correct number and so could stop counting. This discovery has ever since been known as the Clever Hans effect.

This effect was probably understood a lot earlier. A book published in London in 1612 called *The Art of Juggling or Legerdemaine*, says '... nothing can be done [by the horse] but his master must first know, and then by his master knowing, the horse is ruled by signes. This, if you mark at any time, you shall plainly see.'

56   *Thurſday April.* xxvi.

Mr. Sawyer ſaw a horſe once that counted and I wiſhed to trye an experiment with Dodo. Knocking on the wall once, twice, three times and ſo on, I ſpoke aloud the number each time to the Bird, which did not attend until I gave a reward of a ſmall piece of Apple at each knocking. After a good deal of this I forgot to knock as I held up the Apple and Dodo went to the wall and knocked many times with his Beak. I kept on, with this encouragement, ſpeaking the numbers, until to my ſatisfaction the Bird began to match my knocks correctly. I ſaid the number out, three for inſtance, Dodo looked in my Eye a while then knocked three, and onwards to

Thurſday April. XXVI.   57

to nine, making three groups of three. Beyond nine Dodo became uncertayne and fell to arbitrary-neſs.   This great ſucceſs has been repeated, unleſs the Bird is diſtracted or ſullen and ſo long as he gets his rewards. My friends are impreſſed, but full of ſuſpicion that it is a Trick of ſome kind, but I do believe Dodo underſtands numbers. When ſomeone knocks at my door Dodo knocks in kind and runs to my viſitor for food.

Mr. Smythe has made in his Shoppe a harneſs for the Bird to my directions ſo that we can go ſafely walking. We go early, at dawn each day, to avoid unwanted attentions.

E

Gill & Co, Oxford ironmongers

Down an alleyway off the High Street, called Wheatsheaf Yard, you once would have found the firm of Gill & Co, established in 1530. (Wheatsheaf Yard is shown on the last map in **Appendix 10**).

This remarkable pedigree began with generations of the Smythe family, working as ironmongers, as well as brewers and mayors. It was probably Henry Smythe, who was running the business until 1704, that dealt with our diarist.

The firm metamorphosed over the years through the names Bush & Pitcher, Pitcher & Gill, Gill & Ward, until Gill & Co emerged in the 1920s, after swallowing up Barlow & Alden, and Iron, Kidman, & Watts.

They were in the High Street for many years, but in 1952 they moved down the alleyway. They were much loved and relied upon for that particular widget that you might have needed, but sadly ceased trading in Oxford in 2010, after 480 years in business.

Illustrated on the left is a fine lock from one of the doors of the original Ashmolean Museum (now the Museum of the History of Science) in Broad Street. Not by Mr Smythe, but by a Mr Burrows.

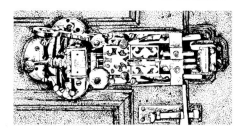

62

Mary's kind ministerings to Mr. Tompkyns arouse the jealousie of my friends. Mr. Sawyer payes fulsome tributes to her beauty, quoting verses and bringing small Gifts. He condescends to talk and jest with her son, only to trye to win her favour. The boy, his name is **Guy**, desires to be with his Mother tho' he lives with his Grandmother at Hinksey, the father being gone somewhere. He is unschooled but shews great gravite, and his Draweings of Dodo, done on the wall, far exceed our own in skill. Mr. Flay is too bashfull to say a word, but sits mooning close by, leaping up to give assistance to Mary when a chance arises.

Hinksey

There are two Hinkseys: North and South. They are villages a mile or so from the centre of Oxford, on its south-west side.

Saturday *April*. XXVIII. 59

Preſſed the Boy, Guy, to do more Draweings, which he does with increaſing confidence, better even than Mr. Tompkyns I think. Now I will have ſomething to ſhew Mr. Aſhmole and tempt his curioſite. The boy is much taken with Dodo, wiſhes to hear of my Experiments and aſſiſts me with the Babye-Houſe for my Landlord's daughter.

It rayned all the day, ſo no work was to be had at New College nor the Muſæum, neither could I take the Bird for the exerciſe of our legs that has become our cuſtom.

Mr. Flay had news of a Great Tremour laſt night at Chipping Norton, laſting ten ſeconds and throwing folk from their beds.

E 2

Baby houses

The earliest recorded doll's houses were made by the Germans and Dutch and were works of art kept in special cabinets for display rather than toys for children. It wasn't until the late seventeenth century that similar houses began to appear in England. They were known as baby houses because at this time dolls were described as babies. Baby houses were usually made for the privileged classes, so it is surprising to find the landlord of an inn commissioning one.

New College

At the same time as the Museum was being completed, New College, one of the wealthiest colleges, was extending its medieval buildings with two handsome wings towards the gardens. New College might have been prosperous, but according to Anthony Wood its Fellows were 'much given to drinking and gaming and vain brutish pleasure'.

Great Tremour

We have not been able to find out anything about this earthquake in Chipping Norton (some twenty miles north-west of Oxford). However, earthquakes regularly occur in England. In the early hours of 23 September 2002 an earthquake centred on Dudley measured 5.0 on the Richter scale, and on 27 February 2008 one at Market Rasen, Lincolnshire, measured 5.2.

64

Physicians
Physicians were at the top of the medical hierarchy, equipped with all the supposed advantages of a University education: theory, logic, Latin, book-learning, and membership of the Royal College of Physicians. Their high fees unfortunately made them unaffordable for most people, or a desperate last resort.

Cupping
This was a mainstay of the physician's practice for thousands of years. It involved placing small heated cups over the patient's skin to form a vacuum that drew the skin up into a blister. Blisters could also be induced by applying an irritant ointment on a plaster. Blisters were then pierced to let out undesirable matter or blood, with the aim of rebalancing the humours and curing the patient. Alternatively, a small incision could be made prior to cupping, the vacuum drawing out the blood into the cup.

The practice has had something of a revival in recent years, judging by the tell-tale circular bruises revealed by the low-cut dresses of some celebrities. It should be performed by a trained practitioner.

The medicines of the Apoth-ecary and the nursing of Mrs. Spott seem to make Mr. Tompkyns no better, so Mr. Sawyer said he would paye from his own Purse (he can stand it) for a Physician to come. It was the very eminent Mr. Scawry who studied the teach-ings of Galen and Hippocrates at Padua. A prickley-natured fellow who complayned of the stairs and refused to enter the room until Dodo was held. He sent Mrs. Spott away in high handed fashion and was disgusted to hear of the prescriptions of the Apothecary.

After a prolonged studie of the Patient, though without touching him at all, he advised Cupping, which an assistant came foreward with

Sunday April. xxix. ♏ 61

with the Glasses to applie, Draweing the corruptions to the surface of the skin, then pricked and scored him where the Glasses had been so that Mr. Tompkyns cried out in a pitiful manner.

Mr. Scawry will come agayne to see what improvement there might be and if further treatments are necessarie. Mr. Tompkyns moaned all the night. We can be sure it is good Medicine, *said Mr. Sawyer*, because it makes him feel worse. *Queſtion:* why does a Bird not have teeth?

E 3

No teeth

Fossil records show that birds did have teeth, but lost them during evolution. In the slow adaptation for flight, birds shed the weight of a jaw with its teeth and muscles, in exchange for a capacious crop and gizzard which did much the same work and also allowed the bird to quickly swallow its food and fly to safety, or to feed its young at the nest. The adapted beak could usually do the work of incisor teeth.

62 *Monday April.* xxx. ○

G uy has done fine new
Draweings of Dodo, from all
fides, fo that Mr. Afhmole may fee
the Bird life-like and be tempted.
I will call on him foon. Why not
tomorrow?

At the Coffee-Houfe, where
I drank a Cordial, I fpoke with
a Dutchman, Mr. Peter Van
Somebody, I forget exactly, who
cutts Letters for the Printers of
the Univerfity, though I think he
faid he was at work, juft now, on
fome Bloomers. I afked him, with
fome caution, if he had perchance
known a fellow-countryman who
kept performing Creatures. He
faid not and then fhewed me from
his pocket a fmall Book of the
fineft Italian printing, made two
hundred

Mr. Peter van Somebody
The Dutchman 'Mr. Peter van Somebody' must refer to Peter de Walpergen, who was brought over to Oxford by John Fell (who was instrumental in establishing one of the best equipped presses in Europe, as well as being Dean of Christ Church and Bishop of Oxford). There is more about Walpergen, Fell, and the cutting of letters overleaf and in **Appendix 9**.

Coffee Houses
Coffee was a drink from the Middle East that became popular throughout Europe during the seventeenth century.

The first coffee house in England was reputedly the one opened in 1651 by Jacob the Jew at the Angel Inn in the High Street, Oxford, where the Examination Schools stand today. In 1654 another opened at the corner of the High Street and Queen's Lane, where there is still one today, and in 1655 Arthur Tillyard, an apothecary, began to sell coffee in the High Street opposite All Soul's College. Tillyards became famous for attracting a notable group of scientists, including Christopher Wren, Robert Boyle, and Robert Hooke, who formed a Chemical Club there which became the nucleus of the Royal Society when its members continued their careers and coffee habit in London.

Monday April. xxx. ○ **63**

hundred years ago; then laughing coarſly told me it was but a Forgerie. It was neatly done, but peering cloſely in it I came acroſs lewd Illuſtrations. I returned it ſtraightway to him and left.

Mr. Flay reads to poor Mr. Tompkyns from his Dreame Book. I was at a Siege or Battle, *he ſaid*, and ſaw a Soldier in bright yellow livery and a white helmet, ſeated in a trench behind a flimſie palliſade of red and white ſtriped wood. He drank from a cup and ſeemed at eaſe.

E 4

Penny Universities

What was the attraction of these early coffee houses? Not just the novel drink, supped from small earthenware or pewter dishes, which for some was 'the all-healing berry', but for others a 'syrup of soot and essence of old shoes'. It was as much for the liberating atmosphere of a place where, for the price of a penny entrance, people of all kinds and classes could sit together and talk freely. They could also read the newspapers and satirical pamphlets, the notices of rival quacks on the wall next to advertisements for house sales, plays and concerts, form societies, smoke their pipes, and collect their post. Some coffee house proprietors would shave you, cut your hair, or draw your teeth; some even put together small libraries or collections of curios.

Time wasting

The appeal of coffee houses for students was obvious. Away from the discipline of their colleges they could enjoy a convivial social life at no great cost, without risking the stigma of taverns or alehouses. No alcohol was sold in coffee houses. If you didn't fancy the coffee you might try chocolate, or sherbet, sassefras, betony, or that other new and much more expensive drink, tea. The university authorities took a dim view of all this time-wasting diversion and suspected seditious plotting. Some futile attempts were made to restrict the coffee houses.

68

Large Bloemen letters

These large floriated letters were specially designed for their decorative qualities, and would usually have been used to start the opening paragraph of a new chapter.

Stanley Morison in *John Fell: The University Press and the 'Fell' types*, 1967, was not able to give the name of their creator. Harry Carter in *A History of the Oxford University Press*, 1975, suggests George Edwards, who gets a mention in the diary page opposite. However, the previous page also puts Peter de Walpergen in the picture.

Fifteen letters of the alphabet have survived and are still at the Oxford University Press (the photograph above shows the letter G). Morison says that these letters were made to a depth of 14 lines of the Pica typesize (equivalent to 12 points x 14 = 168 points). However, on measuring the letters B, I, and G, the block typesize varies from 157 to 190 points.

These beautiful letters only appeared in a few books, for example Anthony Wood's *Historia et Antiquitates Universitatis Oxoniensis*, 1674—a book mentioned in **Appendix 10.**

64

EHOLD Reader, thefe two pages are put in by the Printer of this Book. They were not part of the Manufcript of *A Bird Confidered,* but are added in to fhew our Bloemen Letters, as they are fpoken of on *Monday April.* xxx. I can fay they were engraved on the wood with the fharpeft of tools, to better the Bookes of the Univerfity Prefs.

Small Bloemen letters

As well as the large letters, there was also a smaller version in use at Oxford, sometimes known as Five Line Pica. The letters A and B are shown here, and are referred to in the diary page, above right. Nineteen of the original twenty five letters still exist today, and, like their bigger companions, they were cut on the end-grain of boxwood. A trial proof of the letters soon after they were created is in the Bodleian Library in Oxford and has a note by George Edwards acknowledging receipt of payment from Dr Fell—which confirms that Edwards was their maker.

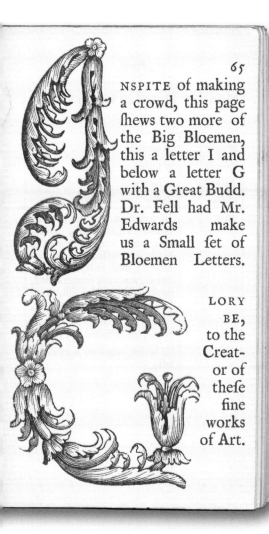

65

NSPITE of making a crowd, this page ſhews two more of the Big Bloemen, this a letter I and below a letter **G** with a Great Budd. Dr. Fell had Mr. Edwards make us a Small ſet of Bloemen Letters.

LORY BE, to the Creator of theſe fine works of Art.

The world of bloomers

The Dutch word 'bloemen' (meaning flowers) was translated into English as 'bloomer', but has had limited use as a term for these kinds of letters. In 1899 MacKail wrote of the 'large floriated initials, or "bloomers", in the slang of the press', and in Watson's *History of the Art of Printing*, Edinburgh, 1713, there is mention of 'Blooming letters'.

There are several other meanings for bloomer in English. There is the core meaning of a plant that blooms, but it can also be used figuratively for a person who is realising their potential, and also in the phrase 'to make a bloomer' or blunder.

The word 'bloomer' is also used for a large white loaf that has angled slashes on its rounded top, but this 'bloomer' is not connected to the 'flower' word, and its origin is unknown.

In the mid-nineteenth century a strong advocate of the women's rights movement in America, Amelia Jenks Bloomer, gave her name to bloomer costume, which is a short skirt and long loose trousers gathered at the ankles. It became very popular. The word was later applied to women's loose trousers (used for cycling, gymnastics, etc.) or women's undergarments reaching down to the knee.

The tradition of ornate flower or leaf-like letters has continued. Here is a typeface designed by the English type designer Eric Gill in 1937 called Gill Floriated Capitals.

70

These pages are similar
to the observations listed
in the diary at the end of
March.

The dodo has put on
several more pounds in
weight, an inch in height,
but fortunately its length
has stayed the same. The
diet is remarkable in its
variety, as is the training that
the diarist has achieved, so
that the dodo responds to
its name being called, etc.

Monthly Digeſt of Obſervacions

Weight	42 pounds
Height	17 inches
Length	12 inches
Colour	darker
Food	In addition to thoſe mentioned before: moſs, whelk, crab, bread, ſcraps of meat of all kinds, eel in jellie, egg (raw and boyled), ſnail, milk, lemon pye, onion, wax cork from a bottel, ſmoked fiſh, pickled fiſh, dryed beans, parkin, chaff, nutmeg, oyſter, anything.
Moult	None, tho' afflicted by Fleas.
Stones	As before, whatever is careleſſly left.

April. 67

Sleepe	From Dufk till Dawn in his basket.
Activitie	Often excited to run about the room, a kind of Dance. Daily taken out to walk on the fields beyond Chrift Church and by the River there, returning by the Phyfic Garden. Will not fwim. Loofed with care it will bring me fticks and not roam far from me.
Refponfive-nefs	Will come to its name, can count, knows fimbols, fome words, likes to be petted.

A stamp from Mauritius

This 12 cent stamp is from the land of the dodo. We looked it up in a catalogue and it shows a portrait of George V, as Mauritius was part of the British Empire at the time, only gaining independence on 12 March 1968.

There were several different versions of the 12 cent stamp printed—some in greyish slate, grey, and pale grey colours—but this is the carmine-red version from 1922. It's not valued at anything very much.

As with so many of the items found interleaved within the diary, it would be good to know how it got here.

Please bear in mind that it is still an act of treason to place a postage stamp bearing the British king or queen's image upside-down on an envelope.

Here is a picture of Dodo's head, drawn from the life when he was docil.

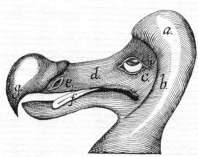

Dodo's Head.   Pag. 69.

M. Burghers ſculp.

a. Gray Feathers. b. Earhole.
c. Eye   d. Light Brown Skin.
e. Noſtril Hole.   f. Tongue.
g. Beak of Horn.

Just as the entries for the end of March in the diary included an image engraved by Michael Burghers, here is another one, this time a finely-detailed dodo's head. The copper-engraving is signed with a note in Latin that M. Burghers *sculpsit* (sculpted it).

Michael Burghers
Michael Burghers (1647/8–1727) was originally from the Netherlands. He arrived in Oxford in 1673, following the French capture of Utrecht during the previous year.

Burghers worked initially under David Loggan, assisting on his great work *Oxonia illustrata* of 1675 (which illustrated the colleges of the University). Thereafter he worked for the University for over fifty years, becoming one of the foremost engravers of his day. In about 1694 he succeeded Loggan to the University post of *calcographus academicus*.

Burghers engraved vast numbers of book illustrations, title pages, portraits, and maps for the University Press, including the first run of Oxford Almanacks from 1676 to 1719.

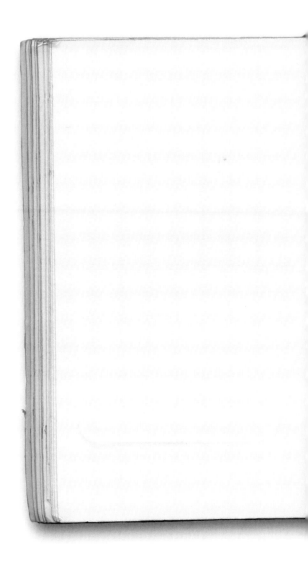

There are no entries for the:

firſt day of May,
ſecond day of May,
third day of May,
fourth day of May,
and the fifth day of May.

READER PLEASE NOTE.

There doesn't seem very much to say about these pages.

Five days ago, the firſt of May, was the day I had reſolved to go on my Viſit to Mr. Aſhmole, to ſhew him the Draweings and the Records of my Obſervacions. I was able to leave Dodo and Mr. Tompkyns in the care of Mary. In my knapſack I had the roll of Guy's Draweings, my Notebook, the Bird's footeprint, and proviſions for the Journey. Of courſe I did not think to take Dodo, for fear of loſing him. Mr. Flay ſurpriſed me by deciding at the final moment that he would come with me, if I did not mind. Indeed I did not, being glad of his Companie and he could vouch for my account of the Bird when we met with Mr. Aſhmole. He would not tell of his

Sunday May. VI. ≋ 73

his going to his Tutor, for fear of another tongue-laſhing.

We left at dawn on May morning, paſſing the Folk gathered under Magdalen's Tower to hear the Choir. There was rude ſingeing and dancing by thoſe who had not ſlept but had drunk too much in the Fields and beſide the Road as far as Shotover. Mr. Flay recounted innumerable Dreames as we went, or perhaps it was one monſtrous long Dreame, of which I now recall only one thing : a dog guarding a giant Pocket Watch.

It rayned and we were ſplaſhed with filthee water by the Flying Coach we could not afford. Mr. Sawyer ſaid he would paye for it but we preferr'd the exerciſe, I

F   told

May morning

It has been the custom since medieval times for crowds to gather at Magdalen Bridge at 6 o'clock on May morning to hear (if the wind is favourable) the choir of Magdalen College sing a Latin hymn to summer from the top of the tower. Afterwards the crowds disperse to big breakfasts, Morris dancing, and other celebrations. The police have had to intervene in recent years to stop dangerous leapings into the river and make the area alcohol-free.

May Day, the first day of summer, has always been rich in customs: the gathering of wild flowers and branches of flowering hawthorn ('may') to decorate houses and maypoles; singing, dancing, and revelry; parades of May queens, milkmaids, and chimney sweeps; and washing your face in May morning dew to improve the complexion. Most of the merry-making was suppressed by the Protestants then revived after the Restoration, and has withered away slowly since. Oxford's May morning is one surviving fragment.

The Flying Coach
This was the stagecoach to London. It may have been flying, but the journey still took about 13 hours and the fare in 1671 was 12 shillings.

78

told him. We had affiftance fome of the way from a Carter but were looked upon with fufpicion moftly by other travellers, as men of uncertayne purpofe.

Refting for the night under my foldier's canvas Tent I had thought to bring, we continued the next day, taking directions, as we approached London, for Lambeth, eventually arriving at Mr. Afhmole's houfe, that once was Tradyfcant's Ark, in the afternoon. The path to the Door was beneath a pair of Great Tufks.

I hefitated to knock, feeing a face at a window looking at me, but it was a ftuffed Creature. After much knocking a Manfervant opened the door. I afked to fee Mr.

Soldier's tent
The soldier's tent and knapsack make us wonder if our diarist once served as a soldier. We know so little about him. We don't know how old he is, or even what his name is.

The Ark
The Tradescant's house and garden, which Ashmole lived next door to and eventually took over, were off South Lambeth Road in London. It was still a largely rural area in the 1680s. The site was cleared for redevelopment with terraced houses in the 1880s. The area once occupied by the famous gardens full of exotic plants and trees brought from all over the world is now beneath Tradescant Road and Walberswick Street.

A mile or so to the north, by Lambeth Bridge and Lambeth Palace, is the disused church of St Mary, now the Museum of Garden History. Here you will find exhibits commemorating the work of the Tradescants and the family tomb. Also in the church, as if even in death he could not keep away from the Tradescants, is Ashmole's tomb.

A pair of Great Tusks
Not tusks, according to another visitor's account, but 'two vast Ribbes of a Whale'.

Sunday May. VI. ≈≈ 75

Mr. Afhmole but was told the Mafter was away from Home and fhould not be expected to return for a Week at the leaft. This was a bitter difappointment.

All that was left for us was to retrace our fteps to Oxford. Surely you muft have written a Letter in advance of your coming, *faid Mr. Flay*. Alas, I had not thought to do fo.

Where was he?
So where was Ashmole at the beginning of May 1683? We looked at his own diary and found that he had been confined to his house for most of the preceding two months. On 25 April he records 'I went first abroad, after so long confinement by reason of my gout'. After that, entries are sparse until September. Of course he might have been at home that day, but didn't feel like seeing anyone.

F 2

Whalebone Arch
There was a tradition of making grand archways from whalebone ribs, such as this one to Netherurd House, near Blyth Bridge in the Scottish Border hills of Peeblesshire.

Here is a plan of my room above-stairs, showing the movements of Dodo, as I took particular note of them, between the hours of 6 o'clock in the morning until mid-day.

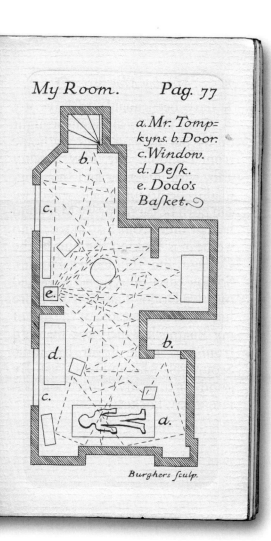

My Room. Pag. 77

a. Mr. Tomp=
kyns. b. Door.
c. Window.
d. Defk.
e. Dodo's
Basket.

Burghers fculp.

The plan

It is fascinating to have this plan of the diarist's attic room, scene of so many of the incidents described. There is no scale provided, although Mr Tompkyn's recumbent figure (assuming he is of an average height) suggests the room had maximum dimensions of approximately 27 by 14 feet.

The eight hours spent by the dodo wandering around the room reveal a much more complicated shape than we had imagined.

The second door marked must be the one leading onto the roof, and the circular shape towards the middle of the room may be the brazier. And is the large rectangle to the right of the brazier the chest used to block the hole into the adjoining chicken and pigeon house?

Incidentally, in the entry for 11 April it is a chest that blocks the hole, but by the 18 April it is a press— a word used at the time for a large shelved cupboard holding books or clothes and probably a more effective obstacle.

82

Ague
An obsolete term meaning a fever characterized by shivering, chills, and sweating. In the seventeenth century this might have been malaria or influenza.

I have been unable to leave my room due to an ague brought on by our difficult Journey home from London. Mr. Flay is fickly alfo, with fhivering and fneezing, glad to be ftopping here where we can both be cared for by Mary and he can hide from his Tutor, who we hear is looking for him in the College and the Coffee-Houfes. So now three of us lie here, walked over by Dodo. I am in truth more hurt than fick becaufe of the lofs of my knapfack which was fnatch'd from me in a ftorm by fome Scoundrels who ambufhed us. By good fortune my Notebook was fafe in my Pocket.

Tuesday May. VIII.   79

Concerned that I am unable to earn my rent I trye to continue at leaſt with the babye-houſe, uſing columns, windows, and door frames from a model of the Muſæum once made for Mr. Wren. I have made for the houſe an attic room juſt like mine and will make furniſhings &c. to match, alſo figures to ſcale of us all: Mr. Tompkyns in the bed, my friends, Mary, Guy, and Mrs. Spott coming in at the door, and Dodo of courſe. Guy is painting the checkered Signe to go above the Inn door. Then I muſt aſk him to do more Draweings of the Bird.

F 4

Museum model
We know Christopher Wren was asked by the Royal Society in 1668 to provide designs for a building to combine the uses of museum, laboratory, and library. That project came to nothing, but might the model being so enterprisingly recycled by our diarist have been made for it? Or is it a model of the Ashmolean Museum as designed by Wren?

Checkered sign
Could this be a clue to the location of our diarist's room? Down an alleyway off the High Street beside Payne & Son, jewellers, is the Chequers Inn. A tavern was built here in 1500 and by 1605 it was known as the Chequers. Oak panelling and a stone fireplace remain from that time.

Before the tavern there was a moneylender's house on the site. A chequered board is the customary sign of a moneylender, originating in the board used by Romans for calculations. The Chancellor of the Exchequer got his name from the same symbol.

In the eighteenth century animals were put on show at the inn, including a camel, a sealion, and a raccoon. There is a legend that soldiers acting for Henry VIII drove a group of monks into a tunnel that once ran under the High Street to the Mitre Inn and blocked up both ends. It is said that the screams of the dying monks can sometimes still be heard.

Our ſpirits are low, and Mr. Sawyer thinks to raiſe them by reciting his lateſt dramatic role over and over, aſking how we like it. Mr. Flay fears that his Tutor has by now written to his Father, who will take him away from the Univerſity. For the while he ſeems to have no more Dreames, but has begun a Diary, in emulation of my own I think. It is full of complaynts and I ſurmiſe many poyntleſs muſings. I did not read it ſecretely, he preſſed it on me.

Dodo's dung

Pigeon dung was valued as a fertilizer, particularly for flowers and fruit (it is rich in phosphorus and nitrogen). Perhaps dodo's dung was even better than pigeon's dung? The landlord might have been able to sell the dung for use in the tanning trade, where it was used to soften hides. It could also be used to make gunpowder and was valued in medicine. Pitch and pigeon dung were applied to the feet of the dying Charles II in 1685, one of the many futile treatments tried by the best physicians in the land.

Thurſday May. x.   81

My Landlord came to collect his Pail of Dodo's dung he treaſures for his vegetables, and to ſee the babye-houſe; he was well pleaſed with its progreſs. I went with him to his Pigeon loft upon the roof, an octagon in emulation of the Theatre, and ſaw his fancy breeds: Shakers, Tumblers, Forktails, Nebuchadnezzars, and more, a remarkable varietie of forms and colours, achieved by careful breeding from one kind. This makes me wonder if I might breed Dodo with a Turkie or a pretty Duck to improve his looks.

I am ſtill weak and in bad Humour.

Theatre

This is another reference to the Sheldonian Theatre, and in particular the octagonal cupola on its top. The one we visit today for its wonderful views is a replacement dating from 1838, which is rather larger than the original (seen in the illustration on page 5).

Cross-breeding

We don't think this would work. They are different species and don't share sufficient chromosomes in their DNA to produce a hybrid. What do you get if you cross a chicken with a duck? A bird that lays down.

Fancy breeds

There are hundreds of breeds of domesticated pigeons today. A seventeenth-century book mentions seventeen. One of those mentioned in the diary, the Shaker, is a kind of Fantail. A Tumbler is also known as a Roller, a bird fond of turning somersaults in the air. A Nebuchadnezzar is perhaps related to the Eastern Carrier, it is a messenger pigeon sometimes called the pigeon of Nebuchadnezzar. The Forktail is not known today. Perhaps it became extinct?

The landlord seems to be more interested in breeding than eating his pigeons. Here are the names of some more fancy breeds: Scandaroon, Tippler, Gimpels, Pouters, Danzig High-Flyers, Clear-Legged Priests, Norwich Croppers, and Runts.

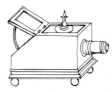

Camera Obscura
It means, literally, 'dark room'. The fifth-century philosopher Mo-Ti first recorded the phenomenon of an inverted image formed by light rays passing through a pinhole into a darkened room. By the sixteenth century, the introduction of a convex lens into the hole and a mirror to project the image onto a viewing surface began to be of interest to artists as well as scientists. Soon a portable box version was developed (see illustration above). Vermeer and Canaletto are among the artists believed to have used such devices.

By the nineteenth century, the Camera Obscura was designed to take a sheet of light-sensitive paper and became a camera. The other development was a small building with a movable lens in its roof which could throw an image down onto a table screen, a popular attraction at beauty spots. Some survive, for example at Edinburgh, Brighton, and Clifton in Bristol.

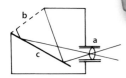

KEY
a lens on a sliding tube for focusing
b ground-glass screen
c mirror

82   *Friday May.* xi. V

Guy does more Draweings of Dodo. There is urgency; what if the Bird ſhould die ſoon, its lively habits and all details of appearance unrecorded? The Boy has quite maſtered Mr. Tompkyn's Apparatus for Draweing, called, Mr. Sawyer believes, a Camera Obſcura, he ſaw one in London, but could not remember how it was uſed. We had looked through its wrong end, and got no help from its owner of courſe. It is a cunning Device and Guy has daſhed off many likeneſſes of the Bird, when it will keep ſtill, and ſome of Mr. Tompkyns who does nothing elſe, and even one of Mr. Sawyer in his new ſkye-coloured and perfumed kidſkin Gloves.

Gloves
Perhaps Mr Sawyer's fancy gloves were made at Woodstock, just outside Oxford, an important centre for glove making (and perhaps pigeon dung was used in the process?).

If they were particularly fancy gloves they were probably imported from the continent, where the craze among the aristocracy for perfumed, dyed, and elaborately worked gloves originated.

Saturday May. xii.   83

About the ſtreets all of the day in ſearch of work, to all the places where I was known, the Maſon's yards, Mr. Petty's Laboratory, the Apothecary Shoppes, Coffee-Houſes to read the bills, to Dr. Plot, even to Mr. Wood, who I do not like, (hearing from him that Mr. Aſhmole will not come next week, he has relapſed into the Gout). Came home weary to diſcover Mr. Flay conducting his own Experiments, concerning Dodo's powers of Hearing. But he was unable to locate the preciſe poſition of the ears.

Mr Petty's Laboratory
If this is William Petty, the scientist (1623–1687), then it's odd that such a laboratory was still in operation in 1683. Professor of Anatomy at Oxford before he was thirty, Petty's old rooms at 106 High Street were a gathering place for scientists such as Wren and Hooke. Petty went to Ireland in 1652 as physician-general to Cromwell's army and afterwards spent most of his time there. Perhaps it's another Mr Petty.

Dr Plot
Robert Plot (1640–1696) was an English naturalist, first professor of Chemistry at Oxford and appointed by Ashmole as first Keeper of the Ashmolean Museum. It was Dr Plot who organized the cataloguing, packing, and transport of the collections from Lambeth to the new museum in Oxford.

Mr Wood
A clue to who this might be is the fact that the diarist does not like him, and he is a last resort. Is it Anthony Wood (1632–1695) the antiquarian who seemed to fall out with everyone? Described as 'a most egregious, illiterate, dull Blockhead, a conceited, impudent Coxcombe', he devoted his life to the recording of Oxford's history. He left his books and letters to the Ashmolean Museum. On the other hand, we must reluctantly admit, it's much more likely to be the master mason, Thomas Wood, already encountered.

Some cigarette cards were found between these pages.

Animalloys

Using one of the handy reference books in Oxford's Westgate library on a blustery late October afternoon, we established that these delightful 'Animalloys' cards were produced in 1934 and given away free in cigarette packets.

They can either be grouped together to make a recognisable animal, or an imaginary one (which is much more fun).

"ANIMALLOYS"

AN UN-NATURAL HISTORY SERIES

48 SUBJECTS — NUMBER 1

This card shows a section of a well-known animal, the sections needed to complete the animal appearing on two other cards. The complete series comprises 16 animals, each in three sections, and by mixing the sections you can produce a large number of strange creatures with amusing names.

W. D. & H. O. WILLS

ISSUED BY THE IMPERIAL TOBACCO CO. (OF GREAT BRITAIN & IRELAND), LIMITED.

and a couple of imaginary animals

Ringing the Bull

This is a very old game, still played today in some pubs. In its most common form a bull's horn is mounted on the wall about six feet off the ground. A ring (preferably one from a bull's nose) hangs from the ceiling six feet or so from the wall, halfway between the thrower and the horn. The object is to swing the ring around the room and onto the horn. Skilled players can perform the double loop, where the ring circles the room completely twice before falling onto the horn on its second loop.

The game probably derives from the brutal and once popular sport of bull baiting. One end of a rope was fastened to the bull's horn, the other secured to an iron ring fixed to a stake in the ground. Dogs were then set on the bull.

The *Trip to Jerusalem* in Nottingham is the most famous pub to still play the game. It's a crusader's tavern, dating from 1189, carved out of the rock under Nottingham Castle.

Microscope

This is the first we've heard of one. Why has it not already featured in our diarist's scientific studies?

84   *Sunday May.* XIII.

Laſt evening we were invaded by Mr. Sawyer and ſome of his ſo-called friends, a rough drunken crew who found their way up from their drinking below; roaring, ſtaggering oafs, who burſt in upon us and chaſed the Bird or ran from it in mock fear, trampelled Mr. Tompkyns, calling for more ale and tobacco. They played at ringing the Bull, though there is no ſpace for it, one of them loſt a tooth. Alſo a kind of ſtick-throwing ſkittles game, breaking bottels and my Microſcope, and miſtaking the Fowle houſe for the Boghouſe. A lewd puppet-ſhew was made of the figures in my babye-houſe before they puſhed Mr. Flay into it. I was angry and made to ejeᶜt them

Aunt Sally

The 'stick-throwing skittles game' must be a form of Aunt Sally. The medieval game called Club Kayles is an early version, in which a stick is thrown at a row of skittles. Stick throwing was a recognized skill, one of its ugliest manifestations being 'throwing at cocks'. This was played on Shrove Tuesday, when a cockerel was the unfortunate target. Another form became popular at fairgrounds, using a wooden cock or human target set up on a stick.

The Aunt Sally pub team game is today largely confined to Oxfordshire and played using six sticks flung at a 'doll' (a skittle) perched atop an 'iron' (a dog-legged metal spike) with the object of knocking the doll cleanly off.

Sunday May. XIII. 8₅

them, but they were beyond all reafoning. Mr. Sawyer was the worft I am forry to fay. How glad I was that Mary and Guy were not here to fee this. At length my Landlord came and got them out with great trouble. One fell from the window with a great crye, while one is ftill here, we found him fpeechleffe drunk in bed next to Mr. Tompkyns.

I am in my Landlord's black bookes. I will have you and your devil Bird out, *he faid*, for all the nuifance you make. He reminded me I am much overdue with my rent.

Black books
Meaning to be in disgrace. Interestingly, at this time in Oxford the Proctors had a black book to record the names of miscreants. No-one whose name was found in the black book would be allowed to take their degree.

Physic Garden
Renamed the Botanic Garden in Victorian times, this is the oldest garden of its kind in the country, founded in 1621 and laid out on land opposite Magdalen College that was previously a Jewish burial ground. It was intended for the study of botany, medicine, and gardening, its formal design dictated by botanical classification.

John Tradescant the Elder was appointed first Keeper of the Garden, but was too ill to take up the post. Jacob Bobart was Keeper from 1642 until his death in 1679. His son, also Jacob, took over, perhaps inheriting his father's goat, an odd choice of pet for a garden full of rare plants.

86   *Monday May.* xiv. ♉

Walked out at dawn with Dodo, as we like to do fo of late, fo as not to drawe unwelcome attention. Acrofs Merton Field and over the wall into the Phyfick Garden where I go naked as Adam along the pathways, naming the plants and Birds (there is a goat) and Dodo can roam free of his reins, though there is no profpect of finding an Eve. On returning my landlord told me he had fhewn my Room to fome men who want it.

Mr. Sawyer is himfelf agayne. He was muddied from playing Foote-ball and faid there was work to be had at the Anatomy School. I could not do that at any coft.

Anatomy School
As early as 1549 medical students at Oxford were required to witness and perform dissections as part of their six years of study for their degree. Lectures and dissections were held at the Anatomy School which was part of the Bodleian Library, and transferred to the Ashmolean Museum when it opened in 1683.

A charter of 1636 permitted the School to demand any unclaimed pauper's body and the body of any person executed within a twenty-one mile radius of Oxford. This sometimes led to violent conflict between medical students and relatives wanting to take the hanged body away for burial. In 1650, Anne Greene, hanged for infanticide, was about to be dissected by William Petty and Thomas Willis when she unexpectedly revived. The doctors pleaded for her and she was pardoned. Apparently, in 1634, a Mr Gosling 'bestowed the Dodar upon ye Anatomy School'. Was this another one? How many dodos were there in Oxford?

Tuefday May. xv. ● 87

Officers of the Univerſity came to ſee us today. We had but a few minutes warning from Mary, allowing Mr. Sawyer and Mr. Flay to make their eſcape over the roof, taking Dodo with them. Six officers with long ſtaves and an Arquebus, and the Marſhall himſelf, made a ſearch of my Room, having had a report of College men where they ſhould not be. They hoped to find cards, dice, bawdy women and led away Mrs. Spott.

I had hid Mr. Tompkyns in the Boghouſe ſo I did not have to explain him.

Arquebus
A muzzle-loaded predecessor of the musket. They had been around for over a century, so this weapon must have been mostly for show. The Marshal was in charge of University officers responsible for discipline, and reported to the Proctors.

94

The Gardener
Could this be Jacob Bobart the Younger? Zacharias Conrad von Uffanbac, a German traveller, visiting the garden some years later 'was greatly shocked by the hideous features and villainous appearance of this good and honest man. His wife, a filthy old hag, was with him, and although she may be the ugliest of her sex, he is certainly the more repulsive of the two.'

But Bobart the Younger was a man who enjoyed a joke. Finding a dead rat in the garden he extended its skin with sticks to give the appearance of wings and presented it as a miniature dragon in so convincing a way that it was displayed for a while in the collection at the Anatomy School.

Fell afleepe as I lay this morning in the Garden, and was chafed out by an angry bearded man, the Gardener I fuppofe. Got away with only fome of my clothes and was injured in the difficulty of climbing over the wall with Dodo under my arm. We cannot go there agayne, I fear.

Mr. Flay continues his Experiments upon the Senfes of Dodo, namely the fenfe of Smell, which he tried to ftudie by blocking of the Bird's noftrills with wax, and his fenfe of Touch, in making him walk upon hot ftones. I ordered him to ftopp thefe cruel tefts.

Mr. Flay dreams agayne. I ſaw
a tall figure of Signs, *he ſaid*.
One Sign was a Shield of three
ſides, and on it was a circle broken
into three parts. Another atop it
had an arrow. Above this a circle
with the number fifty. Over that
a diagonal croſs of red on blue in
a circle. The top moſt ſhield had
three ſides, bordered in red, ſaying
GIVE WAY. It is a target for jouſt-
ing, *ſaid Mr. Sawyer*. Or ſhoot-
ing arrows at, *ſaid Guy*. No, it is
the Arms of a Great Man, *ſaid
Mrs. Spott*, who was releaſed after
rough queſtions. It is a banner
to carry into Battle, *ſaid Mary*.
Mr. Flay did not think it any of
theſe, but a kind of Warning.

G

The Royal visit

A detailed contemporary account of the visit to Oxford of the Duke of York, with his wife Maria and daughter Anne, can be read in *The Life and Times of Anthony Wood, Antiquary, of Oxford, 1632–1695, Described by Himself*. The Duke of York was the brother of Charles II, who he succeeded to the throne as King James II in 1685.

Gloves

Anthony Wood tells us that these were 'a rich pair of gloves with golden fring' for the Duke, 'and to the dutches 12 pairs of fine kid-leather' and for Anne '12 pair also, of the same, all valued at 45 pounds and odd shillings'.

Eastgate

The Eastgate was part of Oxford's medieval city wall where it used to cross the eastern end of the High Street. Today the Eastgate Hotel stands here, on the corner of Merton Street, where the Crosse Sword Inn once stood.

90 *Friday May.* xviii. ♋

A day of great excitement. Went out in the afternoon to join the crowds waiting to greet the Royal Party at the Eaſtgate. Saw the Preſentation by the Mayor of the Gloves, and heard the Latin Oration, when Mr. Sawyer made rude yawns and left to play Foote-ball with the town's people. After the ſingeing and hurrahs for the Duke at Carfax wine poured from the pipes of the Conduit, and ſome were hurt in the ruſh with cups and hats to reach it.

Returning to my room with Mr. Flay, Guy, and Mary, I was diſtreſſed to find the door wide, the Room ranſacked, Dodo gone and Mr. Tompkyns ſtood in a corner, his face a maſk of Horror. I was too

Carfax Conduit

This was the attractive stone structure built in 1610 to receive piped water from the springs at nearby Hinksey. It was positioned at the crossing of Oxford's principal roads, known as Carfax.

The water was passed through the body of a stone ox into two cisterns, one for the University and one for the city. From the conduit further pipes led to colleges and private houses. Most people however still got their water from wells and pumps.

The conduit was superseded by new waterworks at Folly Bridge and was removed in 1789 as it was an obstruction to traffic. It ended up at Nuneham Park, a few miles to the south-east of the city, a sadly eroded exile.

Friday May. XVIII. ♋ 91

too fhocked to act till the children fhouted from their window and pointed their fingers downe into the Alley. I heard Dodo's fkwauk then, diftantly. We haftened downe and heard the Bird once agayne, fo knew the way to give chafe againft the prefs of people coming from the High Street, who hindered us but alfo the two thieves, who we faw ahead of us, one bearing a fack upon his back.

At the High Street thefe men forced their way towards All Saints Church and ran pell-mell paft Lincoln College, downe Brafenofe Lane, where we followed, fhouting Stopp Thief fo that others came with us, or were knocked afide, revellers or dancers, G 2 whoever

You can follow the route of the chase on the maps in **Appendix 10**.

As there is some space left on this page, below is a photograph of one of the pair of pylons that span the River Thames at West Thurrock. They are just downstream from where the Queen Elizabeth II bridge (better known as the Dartford bridge) carries the M25 motorway across the river. They are the tallest pylons in the United Kingdom at 190 metres or 630 feet tall, and were built in 1965 to give a clearance of 75 metres or 250 feet for shipping to pass under the 380 kilovolts powerlines. This photograph was taken from a yacht as it sailed underneath them.

Wine poured from the pipes of the conduit
Such generosity was often a feature of special occasions. In 1660 'a Hogshead of Clarett' was poured into the Carfax conduit instead of water, to mark the Restoration of the monarchy.

Fortifications
The chase must have included what is now Little Clarendon Street and then moved onto the open ground of Gloucester Green. Some of the remains of the Civil War fortifications can be seen on Loggan's map as a wriggling snake shape of raised earth (**Appendix 10**). The map below is from *Alden's Oxford Guide* of the 1880s, although the fortifications may not have been quite as grand as they are shown here.

Between October 1642 and June 1646 Oxford was the military headquarters of Charles I and the Royalist army. Teaching virtually ceased and members of the University were forced to build ramparts, palisades, and ditches around the city. These were flattened by the Parliamentarians after the Royalist surrender of the city.

whoever we met in our path. We went through the Schools, into Broad Street, where there was a crowd playing Foote-ball, among them Mr. Sawyer, and was able to put out his foote to bring one of the kidnappers downe and fat upon him heavily to hearty cheers from all in the chafe. But it was not the man who carried the fack.

With Mr. Flay I kept on at the heels of this fellow, through St. Magdalen's Yard vaulting fences and graveftones, and downe St. Giles. My ftrength from my exercifes told and I was gaining upon my quarry, fure now that I would overhaul him. He turned downe by St. Giles Church onto the old fortifications and over Gloucefter

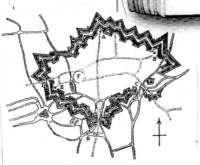

KEY
A   St Giles Church
B   Holywell Church
C   Magdalen Bridge
D   Folly Bridge
E   St Thomas Church
F   Oxford Castle

Gloucefter Green, raifing the angry cries of fome women who had their wafhing laid out upon the Ground to dry; paft Gloucefter Hall, where he ftumbled and almoft fell, to Broken Hayes. Here the weary wretch defpaired and threw downe the fack. I did not follow him further; we had refcued poor Dodo, who was a forry fight indeed, all a-quiver when we got him out of the fack. By now it was evening and the bonfires were lit.

G 3

Gloucester Hall
This was the academic hall that became Worcester College in 1714.

Broken Hayes
This was a recreation area surrounded by trees. It was once used as a bowling green, but had come down in the world to such an extent that Anthony Wood called it 'a rude broken and indigested place'. Hayes is an old word for hedges.

Bonfires
Bonfires were part of the celebrations for the Royal visit in 1683; the biggest of which was at Carfax in the centre of Oxford. That evening the Royal party were lavishly entertained at Christ Church.

This pylon, near Nympsfield in Gloucestershire, is an example of a deviation pylon as it allows the powerlines to turn a corner.

WE CAN'T PUT THIS IN →

These are rare photographs from the early 1930s showing the construction of high-voltage electricity pylons.

The slightly unnerving photograph (top of the next page) with its view from the top of pylon number 103, mentions the River Aire on the reverse. This river's source is near Malham, Yorkshire, from where it travels through Leeds, joins the Calder near Castleford, passes through Rawcliffe to join the Ouse near the village of Airmyn, and finally reaches the Humber and the sea on the east coast of England.

Rawcliffe is mentioned on the reverse of the photograph on the right. The photograph on page 102 mentions Whitely Bridge which is about 10 kilometres or 6 miles west of Rawcliffe.

On the reverse is handwritten:
'Rawcliffe Terminal mast   144'

Looking at the text on the reverse of the other photographs, 144 is probably the number of the tower.

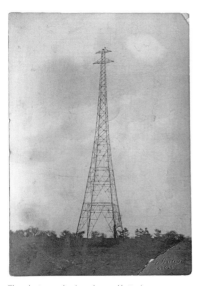

The photographer's embossed lettering 'J. G. Paules, GOOLE' is shown bottom right. There was nothing written on the reverse.

In 1928 the Central Electricity Generating Board had the architect Sir Reginald Blomfield help in establishing the first standard design for a pylon to carry high-voltage electricity cables in the United Kingdom. It was based on a design by the Milliken brothers and later became known as the PL1 and PL1b.

On the reverse of this stunning photograph is handwritten:
'View from top of No 103 looking along conductors   River Aire in background'

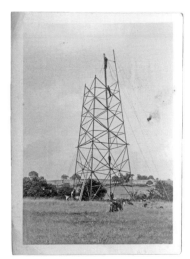

In this photograph there seem to be three figures clinging to the pylon and a fourth at the base. There is nothing written on the reverse.

On the reverse is handwritten:
'Angle tower   No 138.   Y.E.P.C'

Perhaps Y.E.PC. stands for Yorkshire Electricity Power Company? A coat-clad figure clings on.

The Royal tour
On Saturday 19 May the Royal party went on a tour of ten colleges and the Physic Garden, before going by coach to Cornbury Park near Charlbury, home of the Earl of Clarendon, where they stayed until the Monday.

94   *Saturday May.* XIX.

A day of Recovery, not leaſt for our Bird, which though it ſuffered no bodilye injurie has not ceaſed its ſhivering, and keeps to its baſket, taking no food or water.

Sunday May. XX. ♌

Fearful of going out of doors left villains make a new attack. Dodo is in poor ſpirits, feathers beginning to fall out. Mr. Sawyer gave him fine French Brandy.

One more early pylon photograph. On the reverse is written:

'Base of large tower crossing P.O. line near Whitely Bridge mast No 46.
Base 15' square
height 58 feet.'

Fortunately a suitcase appears in the photograph, to help give an idea of scale.

Monday May. xxi.   95

The Royal Companie was entertained at the Theatre and at Afhmole's Mufæum, enjoying a fumptuous Banquet there. A fad mifadventure here meanwhile, when fomeone came up the ftairs and Mr. Sawyer, thinking it a kidnapper, brained him with his ftick as he entered. It was the Phyfician, come to attend Mr. Tompkyns.

More feathers fall.

G 4

Sumptuous banquet
On Monday 21 May the Royal party returned to Oxford and resumed their tour of the University, taking in six more colleges, the Bodleian Library, the Sheldonian Theatre, and the new Museum, where they were entertained by the rarities, a sumptuous banquet, and some experiments in the laboratory. Quite a day.

Parting gifts
On the morning of their departure from Oxford the Royal party were presented with books by the Vice Chancellor. They were Anthony Wood's *Historia et Antiquitates Universitatis Oxoniensis* for the Duke, David Loggan's *Oxonia illustrata* and Dr Plot's *Natural History of Oxfordshire* for the Duchess, and an English bible 'all richly bound and gilt' for the Lady Anne. **Appendix 10** gives some more information about a couple of these books.

96 *Tuesday May.* xxii. ☉ ♍

Mr. Sawyer ſhewed me his Diary, recently begun, ſuppoſedly written by the Bird himſelf; for example: Ate an Apple. Counted to one hundred. Courted a pigeon &c.

We are like priſoners in my room, unwilling to go out and yet made aware conſtantly by my unfriendly Landlord that we are not wanted. I cannot earn a penny in wages and Dodo is falling into a decline, merely taking water that I trickle into his throat.

On the back of this photograph is written:

I'm badly injured but still ¹⁵⁄₁₆ asleep – as usual
Tim   June 1931

Wednefday May. XXIII.   97

A furprifing vifit this day from fome men I took to be wifhing to view my Room, as they were fhewn up by my Landlord. But it was Mr. Afhmole himfelf, who I did not know was in Oxford, carried up by Attendants with confiderable difficulty; he was come to fee the Bird he had heard rumour of. He ftayed an hour talking moft civilly with us, taking great intereft in my Obfervacions, looking over my Notes and Draweings, faying he would like to get them publifhed, they were worthy of bringing to the attention of the Men of Learning over all Europe. I felt dizzie with fo much flattery and fuch profpects of my future. My fine feelings were brought downe

Gout

Ashmole's difficulties with the stairs are evidence of his suffering from Gout.

Gout, or metabolic arthritis, is caused by a build-up of uric acid in the blood, leading to the deposit of uric acid crystals on joints, tendons, and surrounding tissue, causing inflammation and excruciating pain.

Protein-rich food and alcohol were traditionally considered the cause, so in the eighteenth century it became a disease associated with affluence, something of a status symbol. It often first attacks the big toe, as Ashmole discovered.

The Laboratory
As the first keeper of the Ashmolean Museum and University Professor of Chemistry, Robert Plot presided over the running of the building as well as lecturing in Chemistry and founding the Oxford Philosophical Society, where members could 'talke of Chymicall matters'.

The expensively equipped laboratory, with its furnaces, Great Reverbatory, Iron Digester, Alkanor, Alembic, etc., would have been a noisy and smelly place. It shared the museum's basement with a chemical library and a storeroom that was a kind of dispensing pharmacy, where people could go to buy medical preparations.

It is hard to imagine our diarist continuing his observations in such a place. And he would not have wanted to have anything to do with the anatomy room, where the bodies of animals and executed criminals were dissected.

98   *Wednefday May.* xxiii.

downe fomewhat by his keen wifh to buy the Bird from me, offering a ftupendous fum. I thanked him and told him I would confider his offer, having no real intention of parting from Dodo. He preffed me, fuggefting I might be found a pofition in Dr. Plot's Laboratory at the Mufæum and encouragements to further purfue my excellent ftudies with the Bird. I felt weak and almoft gave way, but prompted by Mr. Sawyer's dumb-fhew of fignals and head-fhakings I repeated that I would like to think over his words for a time and reply to him foon. I am to be found at the Mitre, *he faid.*

The Mitre
There has been an inn at the corner of High Street and Turl Street since the fourteenth century. It was one of the great coaching inns during the seventeenth century, running three coaches a week to London.

I am in a great quandrie. I do not want to give up Dodo to Mr. Aſhmole but it ſeems to be the condition for publiſhing my Obſervacions and ſecuring ſuch employment that would put an end to all my worries. How proud my father would be of my advancement! Mr. Sawyer is full of ſuſpicion, being ſure one of the men in the room with Mr. Aſhmole was the ſame he ſat upon in Broad Street; and would he care for Dodo, or be content to let it die and be ſtuffed out for his collection? My friends do not want to ſee Dodo go to Mr. Aſhmole. We talk of how on its native Iſland, in the warm Sun, it might quickly recover its health.

Voyage to Mauritius
This plan seems reckless. We have not had time to research how it might work, even supposing a man and a sick bird could survive a voyage of many months.

Would he go to Holland and try to get a ship to the East Indies that called at Mauritius? Or find a British ship that would take him to the Dutch colony at the Cape of Good Hope and then try to transfer to a Dutch ship from there?

And how would he survive on the island if he got there? Mauritius at this time was a small and failing settlement of Dutch, their slaves, sugar cane plantations, rapidly disappearing forests, and probably no dodos at all.

100   *Friday May.* xxv. ♎

Why fhould I not go with Dodo to Mauritius? After much thought, and knowing that I would never give up the Bird, I reached this fudden decifion, in my fancy feeing him among his fellows, eating the food he was meant to eat &c. My friends were in great excitement, Mr. Sawyer promifing me funds for the Journey. If I go to Briftol I can trye to get paffage on a Dutch veffel. And where better to purfue my ftudies than on Mauritius?

So I am refolved to go, and in fecret, left Mr. Afhmole trye to ftopp me. Mary and Guy are fad and full of fears for me.

Saturday May. XXVI. 101

My friends afk me in earneft to reconfider my decifion, but I am refolute. To pafs the hours until I go I make prefents of the marvellous objects from the Dutchman's Cheft, (which I earlier defcribed) that are too heavy for me to carry, keeping juft the Telefcope for myfelf. Mary affures me fhe will continue to nurfe Mr. Tompkyns till he is recovered. And when I wonder how and where fhe will be able to do this, Mr. Sawyer furprifed me by confeffing he has taken over the Room for himfelf and would have Mary to live in it. I faw how matters ftood and the looks they made to each other. What of his ftudies? *I afked*. I will not take my Degree, *he faid*, but
go

The Dutchman's Chest
This is the first we have heard of any chest, unless it is the one described on 11 April as 'my chest'. If its contents were 'earlier described' it must have been in the missing pages at the beginning of the diary. It is frustrating not to know what these 'marvellous objects' were.

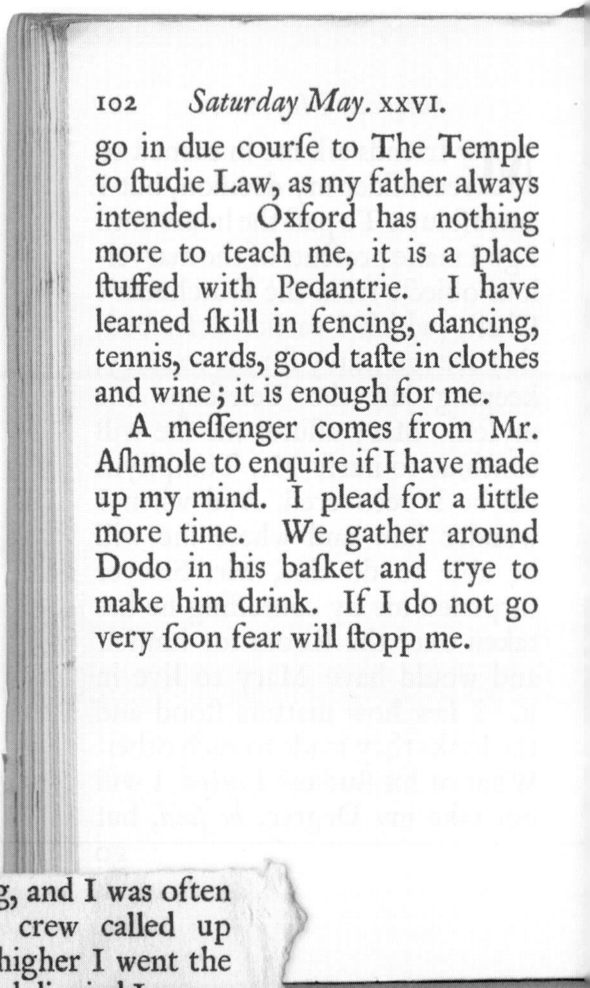

go in due courſe to The Temple
to ſtudie Law, as my father always
intended. Oxford has nothing
more to teach me, it is a place
ſtuffed with Pedantrie. I have
learned ſkill in fencing, dancing,
tennis, cards, good taſte in clothes
and wine; it is enough for me.

A meſſenger comes from Mr.
Aſhmole to enquire if I have made
up my mind. I plead for a little
more time. We gather around
Dodo in his baſket and trye to
make him drink. If I do not go
very ſoon fear will ſtopp me.

A torn diary page?
Sandwiched between these
pages was the singed text
fragment shown below.
At first we believed it to be
from the start of the diary.
However, the glimpses of
subject matter suggest that
our diarist is describing life
aboard a ship, perhaps one
bound for Mauritius, from
one of the later volumes.
We must conclude that at
least one of the four further
volumes mentioned on the
title page was published.
This is an exciting discovery!

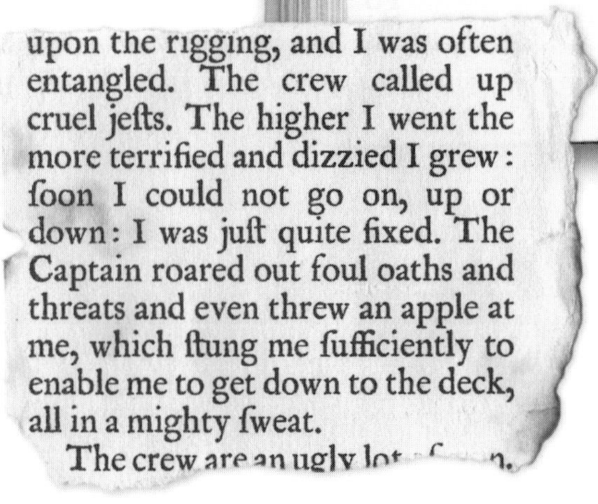

upon the rigging, and I was often
entangled. The crew called up
cruel jeſts. The higher I went the
more terrified and dizzied I grew:
ſoon I could not go on, up or
down: I was juſt quite fixed. The
Captain roared out foul oaths and
threats and even threw an apple at
me, which ſtung me ſufficiently to
enable me to get down to the deck,
all in a mighty ſweat.
The crew are an ugly lot ͡ ͡ ͡ .

Sunday May. XXVII. ♍ 103

Hasty preparations were made through the night for my Expedition, achieved with the kind help of my friends. I will take a covered basket to carry Dodo in, my knapsack with my Tent and a change of clothes. I will give to Mr. Flay my Diary to keep safe to see if Mr. Ashmole will still be desirous of publishing it when he finds me vanished. I can begin another on my travels. Mr. Sawyer has presented me with a handsome sum to start me on my way. I would only waste it on fine apparell and wine, *he said*.

When the time came I said my sad farewells. Mary, Guy, and Mrs. Spott were there to see me on my way and pet the Bird for a last time;

The Diary

What then was the fate of the diary? Did Mr Flay hand it over to Ashmole or did the diarist return and prepare it for publication himself?

There is, after all, a delay of twelve years before the publication of the first volume in 1695. Presumably, if there really were four further volumes of the diary, our diarist must have survived his adventure and made further observations.

Did the dodo survive? Only if and when those lost volumes reappear will we learn the answers to these questions.

time; Mr. Tompkyns made me a kind of ſalute. I promiſed to ſend word when I reached Mauritius, God willing. I go by the next Coach, in one hour.

Theſe are the final words I write before beginning my Journey and a new Diary.

———

FINIS.

———

AN

'Finis' is a Latin word meaning 'the end'.

An Alphabeticall Index of *A Bird Confidered.*

H

The index

As well as covering the diary pages themselves, the index also includes references to the first few pages of the book (known as the 'prelims' or 'preliminary matter') in entries such as 'Aldrich' on page ii.

Intriguingly, there are also entries to words on the missing pages 1 to 6, for example 'Abacus' on page 3. So although the first six pages are missing, we know that they contained the following words: Abracadabra, Abacus, Amulet, Arsenic, Ashmole, Aye, Backslash, and Bob.

A dog-eared page

This term usually means the corner of a page creased or turned over by a reader, so that they can keep their place when they next come back to read the book.

Here, however, it means something slightly different. Sometime between the printing and folding of the sixteen-page signature (see **Appendix 7**) and the binding of the book in 1695, a corner of the paper was mistakenly folded in on itself. The book was then trimmed as part of the binding process which would have left this and the next page connected. When the first person came across it, they would have had to cut open the folded corner.

This is how the diary has ended up with such a strange-looking extension to the corner of the page. After photographing this and the next page, we folded the dog's ear back inside the book, to stop it being damaged.

Missing pages from Index
Unfortunately the remaining twelve pages of the index have been ripped out of the diary.

And here is the other side of the dog-eared page.

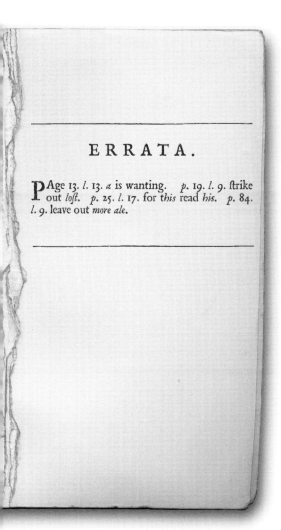

ERRATA.

PAge 13. *l.* 13. *a* is wanting.   *p.* 19. *l.* 9. ſtrike
out *loſt.*   *p.* 25. *l.* 17. for *this* read *his.*   *p.* 84.
l. 9. leave out *more ale.*

Errata slip

The moment after a book
is printed, if there are any
mistakes they become
much easier to spot.
Judging by the binding and
the similar paper quality of
this page, it looks as if the
Errata slip was added just
after the rest of the diary
was printed.

The first entry probably
translates as: on page 13,
line 13 from the top, the
word 'a' is missing. It looks as
if it should be inserted after
the word 'be'.

The brown discolouring of the edges of these endpapers was probably caused by the leather binding. So, although the leather has gone, the book must have been intact for many years before it was removed.

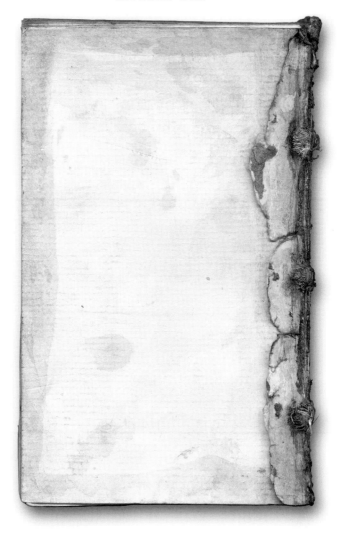

Photographs

Here are a few photographs of the diary. Above is the spine of the book, showing the page signatures and how they are bound together, which would normally be hidden by the leather binding. Below left shows the view from the top, and below right the view from underneath.

APPENDICES

—

W E HAD HOPED to avoid having a set of appendices to this book. However, the lack of space to discuss the diary in detail meant that we changed our minds. We hope that they will be entertaining, as well as informative.

APPENDIX I

Time

There are some strange things going on with time in the diary, which we need to talk about. The page preceding the title page cannot make up its mind which year it is—it says that it is both 1694 and 1695—whereas the title page says only 1695.

We looked at some calendars from the 1690s and they mentioned the new year beginning on 1 January, but this didn't become official in England until the middle of the following century. Prior to that the Julian calendar was still in use, which meant that 25 March was the first day of the new year.

The Ancient Romans began their year on 1 January. From the twelfth century the influence of the Christian Church resulted in the Annunciation of the Blessed Virgin Mary (or Lady Day), which falls on 25 March, being more frequently used in England. The date on the title verso of 1694/5 reflects both these possibilities. If the diary had been printed a couple of months later, say in May, then it would have been dated simply 1695.

The Julian calendar was replaced by the current Gregorian calendar in England in 1752. It was adopted due to the fact that the Julian calendar assumes 365.25 days between vernal equinoxes, when in fact it is about 11 minutes less. In order to move to the more accurate Gregorian calendar, it was ordered that the eleven days of 3–13 September 1752 should be omitted, and that the start of the year be altered to the more familiar 1 January. So 1751 began on 25 March, but 1752 began on 1 January, which meant that 1751 consisted of only 282 days. When King Charles I was executed on 30 January contemporary documents recorded it as happening in 1648, but the Gregorian calendar has since been retrospectively imposed on the event, so that it is now usually stated as happening in 1649.

An Oxfordshire election held in 1754 gives some evidence of dislike to the change of calendar. The Whig candidate, Lord Parker, was the son of the principal backer of the Calendar Act and so was attacked on the issue by his Tory opponents. The cry from the crowd ran 'Give us back the eleven days we have been robbed of'. The animosity between the two parties that produced this strange battle cry would not normally have arisen, as previous elections were uncontested. Usually there was a tacit agreement whereby the Tories stood unchallenged for the shire seat and the Whigs stood uncontested for the boroughs.

Some people thought of the change to the calendar as a Catholic plot, as the Gregorian calendar originated with a decree from Pope Gregory XIII. When he introduced the change in October 1582 ten days were removed, but by the time of the change in Great Britain eleven days were needed to catch up.

The start of today's financial year still harks back to the new year having begun on 25 March, once you add the eleven days from the calendar change (to give 5 April) and add a Julian leap day in 1800, moving it to the familiar 6 April. In 1900 there was a further Julian leap day which should have moved the date to the 7 April, but it was not adjusted, and the date has remained at the 6 April ever since. We should remind readers who have overdue tax returns of the importance of dates to HM Revenue & Customs.

APPENDIX 2

———

When was the diary written?

W e may know when the diary was published, but when was it written? The entry for 25 March fell on a Sunday, so after looking at some calendars for the period, the possible years are 1694, 1688, 1683, 1677, or earlier.

We next checked the moon and zodiac signs that appear at the top of some of the diary entries (see Appendix 4). The University of Oxford has published an almanack with this information continuously since 1676. There had been a few almanacks before that date—the one in 1673 was ridiculed for its inaccuracies, and prompted a satirical ballad entitled 'A Hue and Cry after Good Friday lost in the Oxford Almanack'. Assuming that the almanack is reliable, it suggests that the only year that fits the diary is 1683. The accounts in the diary of the royal visit to Oxford and the opening of the Ashmolean Museum, both confirm the date as 1683.

Most diaries are written within a day or two of the events that they describe, but it is also possible that notes were taken and written up much later on. However, there is an immediacy and liveliness about the text that suggests it was completed soon after the events. It is also possible for the diarist to have gone back over the text and made some changes in preparation for publication. Evidence that the diary was little altered is suggested by the title page dedication to 'Mr A - - - - - - ', which is presumably Elias Ashmole, and subsequent disparaging remarks about him (in such entries as 19 April, 6 May, and 25 May).

When the diary came to be printed, it would be usual for the printer to impose a house style and make editorial changes. Without the original diarist's manuscript to compare against, we won't know how much changed. The missing pages near the start of the diary may have contained notes by the editor or printer explaining the context. Sadly, those pages are missing.

Events in the late seventeenth century

Assuming that the diarist was in his early twenties when he was penning the diary in 1683, he would have been born roughly at the end of Republican government in England in 1660. The Common-wealth had begun in 1648/9 (see the note on time in Appendix 1 about this curious date) with a declaration 'that the people are, under God, the original of all just power', rather than the monarch. However, weakness among the Republican factions lead to the Restoration of the British monarchy and Charles II's reign from 1660 to 1685.

Charles II's brother, James II (also James VII of Scotland) took over as king from 1685 until 1688, but his Catholicism, as well as attempts to rule without consulting Parliament, led to the Glorious Revolution. William of Orange, a Dutch prince, was installed as William III, alongside his wife Mary II (daughter of James II and VII). She reigned until 1694, and he until 1702.

Other notable seventeenth-century events included England being at war three times with the Dutch Republic (1652–54, 1665–67, and 1672–74), resulting in an increased control of international trade for the English. The year 1665 saw the last Great Plague of London, which was followed by the Great Fire of London the next year. In 1683, the same year in which the diary was written, the River Thames froze over, allowing a frost fair to take place in London.

APPENDIX 3

The long s (sſ)

A careful study has been made by the editors of the long 's' character. It is often used in the diary, but does take a bit of time to become familiar.

Up until about the year 1800 there were two forms of lowercase s in use. One form was the s we use today; the other is called the long s and looks like this ſ, which is similar to a lowercase f, but without the right-hand crossbar. The italic form of the long s usually has no crossbar ſ.

The long s was used at the beginning, or in the middle of a word; the short s for the end of a word. So, for fun, here are some examples to practise with:

sassiness → ſaſſineſs

Noun of sassy—a colloquial word for cheeky, or impudent.

scissors, paper, and stone → ſciſſors, paper, and ſtone

The ancient Chinese game in which two players shoot out a hand which is either in a fist (meaning a stone), with two fingers showing (meaning scissors), or lying out flat (meaning paper). To decide the winner: scissors cut paper, paper wraps stone, and stone blunts scissors.

spissness → ſpiſſneſs

From the obsolete word spiss, meaning dense or compact.

and now to combine the long and short s with two examples of
an f:

stiffupperlippishness → ſtiffupperlippiſhneſs

*Colloquial, originally denoting the quality of being unyielding
or stoical, now more generally used in a derogatory way about the
behaviour and attitude of the aristocracy.*

Hopefully the similarities of the long s and the lowercase f are
waning, and the two characters now sit like chalk and cheese upon
the page, rather than identical twins in a poorly lit room.

It is important to recognize the part played by François-
Ambroise Didot, in Paris, in the abandonment of the long s. In 1782
he had a new style of typeface cut, and at the same time abolished
the use of the long s in his printing. This quickly caught on, and
in London, John Bell abandoned the long s in his newspaper *The
World*, first published in 1787. The new convention was quickly
adopted around the country.

APPENDIX 4

Astrological signs

S trange-looking symbols sometimes follow the dates that appear at the start of
each diary page. One set of symbols shows
the phases of the moon and the other is the
signs of the zodiac.

The moon signs

The diary entry for the 25 March shows that the moon was in its
first quarter (☽), then became a full moon on the 31 March (○).
On the 8 April it moved to its last quarter (☾), and on the 16 April
it was a new moon (●). The symbols for the first and last quar-
ters show a lot more of the reflected part of the moon than in the
modern font we use here. For example, the first quarter has two-
thirds in white, compared to a third here (☽). The angle of the
moon changes as it makes its daily progression around the sky—it
is just convention to use a vertical axis.

Our calendar month approximates to the precise time that
the moon takes to orbit the earth, which is 29 days, 12 hours,
44 minutes, and 2.98 seconds, give or take a bit, here and there.

The zodiac signs

The Sun, Moon, Mercury, Venus, Mars, Jupiter, and Saturn all move within a narrow band in the sky, and their relative position to each other and the Earth is the basis of astrology. This is called the zodiacal band and lies within about eight degrees of the average plane of the Earth as it orbits the Sun (called the 'ecliptic').

The zodiacal band is divided into twelve equal parts and each has its own astrological sign which is believed to influence or reflect human activity. In Western astrology each division is linked to a constellation (a group of stars that form a recognized pattern in the sky) and is influenced by the passage of the sun, moon, and planets through it. When a person is born it is important which zodiac sign is appearing on the eastern horizon. The Earth's axis has altered over time, so that now the zodiac signs correspond more closely to the preceding constellation, and the ecliptic has since gained a thirteenth constellation.

The 25 March diary entry shows the sign for Cancer ($\mathfrak{S}$), and the entry for 31 March shows Libra ($\Libra$).

$\Aries$	Aries, the Ram	$\Taurus$	Taurus, the Bull
$\Gemini$	Gemini, the Twins	$\mathfrak{S}$	Cancer, the Crab
$\Leo$	Leo, the Lion	$\mathrm{M\!\!\!\!V}$	Virgo, the Virgin
$\Libra$	Libra, the Scales	M	Scorpio, the Scorpion
$\Sagittarius$	Sagittarius, the Archer	$\Capricorn$	Capricorn, the Goat
$\Aquarius$	Aquarius, the Water-carrier	$\Pisces$	Pisces, the Fish

See Appendix 9 for information on the Pica size of type used for setting the moons and zodiac signs in the diary pages.

APPENDIX 5

Ligatures

Since the start of letterpress printing in Europe in the middle of the fifteenth century it was usual to create ligatured characters in a typeface. In letterpress printing, a ligature is two or more letters cast on a single piece of metal type, and overcomes the technical problem of fitting these letters closely enough together. Ligatures usually have their letterforms joined together (for example ffi instead of ffi), and sometimes a special stroke is added (for example ct instead of ct).

Without a ligature, letters such as ffi can appear unevenly spaced, such as: Griffin, whereas the ligatured version is: Griffin. The metal type for the two approaches is shown below (please note that the letters are back-to-front, so that they print the right way round):

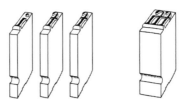

Some of the ligatures we've spotted being used in the diary are combinations with a lowercase f (ff fi fl ffi ffl), long s (ſſ ſi ſl ſſi ſſl ſt), and the lowercase ct (ct).

APPENDIX 6

Kerning

In letterpress printing, kerning is a term that refers to the sideways projection of the face (the part that carries the ink) of a piece of type. It enables two characters to appear more closely together on the printed page. Instead of all of the surface of the letterform sitting within the body of the type, part of it overhangs. For example, the letters V and A without kerning are spaced: VALLEY but they can be kerned to give more even spacing: VALLEY. The kerned metal type would have looked like this (arrows show the overhang):

 and when typeset look like this:

Unfortunately, type that is kerned is more difficult to make and is more easily damaged in use. The letters f and j are often kerned, as well as many italic letters (due to their sloping design). Using ligatures helped to reduce the need for kerning. At the diary entry for 1 April, in line 7 of the text, the word 'ſore head', is an example of a long s that has been damaged at the top of the letterform, which was a common problem.

APPENDIX 7

Page signatures

Many pages in the diary have a code number at the foot of the page, for example, 'B' on the second part of the 23 March entry. These codes run in the sequence B, B2, B3, B4, C, C2, C3, C4, D, D2, D3, D4, etc., throughout the book, but do not appear on every page. They are page signatures, which are markers used to help the printer and binder get the pages in the correct sequence. The first time a letter appears it does not have a number—it is the start of the signature.

Page signatures are needed because groups of pages are printed at one time—typically sixteen, thirty-two, or sixty-four pages. The sheet of paper is then folded and bound with other signatures to make up a book. Opposite are three signatures of sixteen pages each.

Each change of letter indicates the beginning of a new signature. In the diary this happens every sixteen pages ('B' begins on page 9, 'C' on page 25, and 'D' on page 41).

A sheet of paper is printed both on the front and back, so there are eight pages to view on one side and eight pages on the other. The following diagram shows the sheet of paper with the page numbers (called 'folios') and page signatures marked; this is called the 'imposition'. It enables the printed pages to appear in their correct sequence after folding. Why not have a go at making a signature to see how this works?

In the diary there are four page signatures for each signature, and they appear on right hand pages (called 'rectos'), for example B

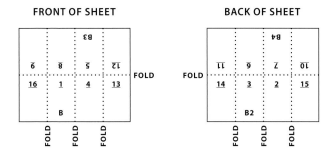

FRONT OF SHEET

| 6 | 8 | 5 | 12 |
| 16 | 1 | 4 | 13 |

B3 · B · FOLD · FOLD FOLD FOLD

BACK OF SHEET

| 11 | 6 | 7 | 10 |
| 14 | 3 | 2 | 15 |

B4 · B2 · FOLD · FOLD FOLD FOLD

on page 9, B2 on page 11, B3 on page 13, and B4 on page 15. Rather than include a page signature for every recto page in this example (B5 to B8), it is usual to only do this for the first half of the signature, as the rest are implied.

Near the beginning of the diary, five leaves (or ten pages) have been carefully cut out from after the title verso page and before the diary entry for 22 March (on page 7). Traditionally, the preliminary pages in a book are separately numbered with Roman numerals (i, ii, iii, iv, etc.), and the main section with Arabic numerals (1, 2, 3, 4, etc). The first sixteen-page signature of the diary begins with the four preliminary pages that survive, and ends on page 8. This suggests that there were four further preliminary pages, and then the beginning of the main section. The first page signature letter 'A' did not usually appear on the printed page in these sorts of situations, because the preliminary pages are easier to get in the correct order and the letter would distract the reader.

The diary has a total of 128 pages, made up of eight signatures of sixteen pages each.

APPENDIX 8

—————

Diary page size

We measured the page size of the diary at about 5 inches tall by 3³/₁₆ inches wide (127mm by 81mm). Appendix 7 established that signatures of sixteen pages each were used, but what was the sheet size of paper used to print the signature? A sixteen page signature has eight pages to view on one side of the paper and eight on the other. So we multiplied the paper height (5 inches) by two, and the page depth (3³/₁₆ inches) by four, which gives 10 inches by 12¾ inches. The sheet of paper has to be a bit bigger than this, in order to allow for trimming during the binding process. The fore-edge margin (the edge of the book furthest from the spine) looks a bit cramped, which suggests it might have been rebound, thereby losing a bit more of the paper.

The Pott paper sheet size of about 12½ inches by 15½ inches (318mm by 394mm) seems the most likely contender; it was the smallest size in common use. There are records of the University Press purchasing stock of it, for example in the Warehouse-Keeper's accounts for 1692. Oxford was fortunate in having good transport links via the River Thames, and a papermill close by at Wolvercote.

The Pott size of paper refers to its watermark depicting a pot, and dates back to the sixteenth century (other delightfully named paper sizes include Crown, Foolscap, and Elephant). The paper used in the diary does not appear to have any watermarks, which otherwise might have given some useful clues to its origin.

If a sheet of paper is folded once it is called 'folio', twice 'quarto', and three times 'octavo'. So the book format of the diary is likely to have been 'Pott octavo'.

APPENDIX 9

Types used in the diary

With today's computers, type can easily be set at whatever size is needed, but when the diary was printed each size had to be individually made in metal. The process was a costly and difficult one, which limited the range of typesizes that were created. Today the size of type is usually measured in points, but in the seventeenth century each size had a special name, such as Canon, English, or Pica.

After referring to Stanley Morison's *John Fell: The University Press and the 'Fell' types*, 1967, we spotted the following types used in the diary.

> Fourteen Line Pica Decorated Initial Letters (about 168 point)
> Two Line Double Pica (about 40 point)
> Canon (about 40 point)
> Two Line English (about 27 point)
> Double Pica (about 20 point)
> English (about 13 point)
> Pica (about 12 point)
> Long Primer (about 9 point)

John Fell and the 'Fell' types

The types used in the diary are known as the Fell types, named after John Fell (1625–1686), Dean of Christ Church and Bishop of Oxford. He was largely responsible for setting up and maintaining a prestigious scholarly press at the University, after looking to France and Holland for inspiration, expertise, and types. The press became one of the best-equipped in Europe and produced many beautifully designed books. Fell was not the designer of the types, but was instrumental in purchasing and commissioning them. He established the press in the University's Sheldonian Theatre (designed by Christopher Wren) which opened in 1669.

Fell stocked the press with many different types so that not only English and Latin, but Greek and many exotic scripts could be typeset and printed. These types were mostly sixteenth-century French or seventeenth-century Dutch in origin. Many were bought by Dr Thomas Marshall during two trips to Holland in 1670 and 1672. These included the English, Pica, and Long Primer types used in the diary.

Marshall actually purchased matrices, which are the moulds from which type can be cast whenever it is needed. It was better to have the means to cast type rather than rely on buying new type from an outside type foundry. A few years later Fell went one better and employed a punchcutter to create new designs by engraving punches, from which matrices were struck, and then type cast. The letter on the punch is cut back to front, so that it is the right way round on the matrix, then the wrong way round on the type, and so appears correctly on the printed page. Peter de Walpergen almost certainly cut the Canon, Double Pica, and the astrological, mathematical, and number signs in the Pica size for Fell.

If Fell is remembered it may well be for the unkind epigram by Thomas Brown:

> I do not love thee, Dr Fell.
> The reason why I cannot tell;
> But this I know, and know full well,
> I do not love thee, Dr Fell.

Fell bequeathed his material from the press to the University on his death in 1686, and it was formally taken over by the University in 1690. This marked the uncontested establishment of the Oxford University Press, which still holds Fell's types in its rich archive.

Peter de Walpergen, letter founder

Harry Carter's *A History of the Oxford University Press*, 1975, contains plenty of information about Peter de Walpergen, who was a Dutch letter founder, of German origin. He had worked in the

Dutch East Indies before being persuaded to move to Oxford by Fell in 1675 or 1676, where he worked until his death in 1703. He was paid £36 a year (later rising to £40), plus his 'diet'. He worked in the Dean's lodgings at Christ Church, where he also waited on Fell's table when there were visitors. Records survive showing that Walpergen was sued four times in the Chancellor's court of the University for debts to tavern-keepers and cooks. He is mentioned in the diary entry for 30 April.

Walpergen produced sixteen complete types for Oxford, as well as additions and replacement characters for existing ones, such as modernizing the English type—the most frequently used type in the diary. His name was variously spelt as Peter de Walpergen, Pedro Walberger, Petter de Walpergen, and Mr Warborough. Could this multitude of names be less to do with the relaxed attitude to consistent spelling in his day, and more to do with the need for multiple pseudonyms to avoid debts to tavern-keepers and cooks?

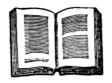

The types in detail
Below is some information about the history of each type, and examples of where to spot them in the diary, beginning with the largest size.

• **Fourteen Line Pica Decorated Initials** (about 168 point)
This was the largest size of letter available at the press, and for technical reasons was made in wood, rather than metal. The three letters 'B I G' appear in the diary on the two pages following the 30 April entry. They were probably carved in Oxford, and there is further information about them alongside those diary pages, and in the notes beside the 30 April entry itself.

- **Canon** (about 40 point)

This is the largest of the metal types and has also been called Oxford Canon, French Cannon, Great Cannon, Three Line Pica, and Two Line Paragon. It is used on the title page to set the word 'BIRD' and has an elegant and slightly quirky feel. Punches and matrices survive in the archives of the Oxford University Press. The type first appeared in print in 1686 and it was almost certainly created by Walpergen.

- **Two Line English** (about 27 point)

Appears in the diary entries as the initial letter of an opening paragraph. It was bought in London in 1695. The Roman was probably cut by Dirk Voskens of Amsterdam, and the Italic by Nicholas Kis, who was originally from Transylvania and studied under Voskens. No punches, matrices, or type have survived at the Oxford University Press.

- **Double Pica** (about 20 point)

Appears on the title page for the words 'A' and 'CONSIDERED', as well as on the following page for the wording 'Imprimatur, Henr. Aldrich'. This was the first of the Latin types cut by Walpergen for Fell at Oxford and it was first seen in print in 1682. Punches and matrices survive.

- **English** (about 13 point)

This is the principal type used in the diary entries. It also appears on the title page and the page following it, and is used for the catchwords, page signatures, and running headlines. According to Morison, the Roman type has been found in use in Amsterdam as early as 1635, and was probably cut by a French emigrant as it combines the Parisian mid-sixteenth-century style of Claude Garamond, with the straighter lines of the mid-seventeenth-century Dutch style. It is recorded that 141 matrices were purchased of the Roman from Holland. The origin of the Italic is unknown, but it appeared in the second quarter of the seventeenth century in Holland. The 118 matrices for the Italic were also purchased in Holland by Marshall.

It was decided to modernize the design by replacing several characters (eighteen letters in the Roman and eight in the Italic), which were cut by Walpergen. This new version first appeared in an Oxford book printed in 1688, and became standard from 1691 onwards. The diary uses the modernized version.

- **Pica** (about 12 point)

This type appears on the title page and the page following it. There were two versions of the Pica size in use at the press. The first one was purchased in 1672, for which 153 matrices survive for the Roman (perhaps cut by Claude Garamond in Paris in the mid-sixteenth century) and 128 matrices for the Italic (cut by Robert Granjon, also in Paris, and at the same period).

Walpergen cut a second Pica type, which was used at the press from 1692, but this is not the one seen in the diary.

• **Pica astrological, mathematical, and number signs**
The astrological signs appear towards the start of each diary entry, following the date. Punches and matrices, which Walpergen cut, survive and appear in a 1693 type specimen. Amongst the mainly mathematical signs, were also two moons, which appear after the date in the diary entries. The new moon and last quarter moon are shown in a 1695 type specimen, but not the full moon and first quarter moons that appear in the diary. There is also a set of cancelled numbers and fractions (these are used on the title verso page). The signs were probably commissioned specially for John Wallis's *Opera mathematica et miscellanea* of 1693.

• **Pica Ornaments** (about 12 point)
There are two ornaments used for the opening page of the month of April in the diary. They were cut by Walpergen and appear in the 1695 type specimen. Punches and matrices survive.

• **Long Primer** (about 9 point)
This is used for setting the monthly observations and the text of the index, as well as a fleeting use on the title page. The type was purchased in 1672. The Roman had 153 matrices, punchcutter unknown, but many letters were in use by 1558. The punchcutter Christoffel van Dyck may have been responsible for modernizing it. It first appears in use at Oxford in the Bible and Book of Common Prayer published in 1675. The Italic was cut by the same Christoffel van Dyck, and 121 matrices were brought to Oxford.

As well as type for setting letters, music type also appears in the diary.

• **Two Line Double Pica Music** (about 40 point)
Music appears between the entries for the 4 April and 5 April. The type may well have been commissioned by Henry Aldrich, Vice Chancellor of the University, who is mentioned on the page preceding the title page (where there is also a note in the margin about him). The University bought the music type in 1694 from Walpergen, and it first appeared in a type specimen in 1695. The famous diarist Samuel Pepys was sent a proof, as a letter from him survives dated 1694 referring to the 'musick-characters'. It has been claimed that the music type is Walpergen's masterpiece.

APPENDIX 10

Maps of Oxford

The following pages reproduce one of the finest engraved maps of the city of Oxford ever made. It shows not only streets and lanes, but buildings, trees, waterways, vegetable patches, sheep, civil war fortifications, and even a weathervane (not something you see very often on a map today).

David Loggan's bird's-eye view of Oxford was published in 1675 and looks from the north towards the south. It was one of the plates created for *Oxonia illustrata*, that also included views of all of Oxford's colleges, academic halls, and university buildings. The diary was written a few years later, so little had probably changed for our diarist as he walked around Oxford's streets.

Following on from the illustration of the complete Loggan map is a close-up of the central area of Oxford. This shows more clearly where the diarist lived (just off the High Street), and the route of the Dodo chase. Further on still, are a couple of modern-day maps, for comparison, that mark these locations.

David Loggan, map-maker

David Loggan was born in Poland, of a family of Scottish merchants, in the early 1630s. He studied engraving in various cities on the continent, before settling in London. Impressively, he not only drew Oliver Cromwell during the period of Republican government in Britain (1649–1660), but later made the transition to portraits of the restored monarch, Charles II, and many in his court.

In order to escape the London Plague of 1665 he and his wife moved to Oxfordshire. He had many commissions from the University of Oxford and in 1669 was appointed its engraver, probably through the support of John Fell (the same John Fell who purchased many of the types used in the diary). Loggan was paid a token fee of 20 shillings (one pound) a year, which is worth the equivalent of about £130 in today's money.

In 1675 he printed *Oxonia illustrata*, which contains the following map of Oxford. It was printed entirely from engraved plates in David Loggan's house, selling for about one pound a copy. It was often bought or presented alongside Anthony Wood's *Historia et Antiquitates Universitatis Oxoniensis,* 1674, which documented the University's history.

In 1675 Loggan moved to London. Amongst other work, he later engraved images of the Cambridge colleges and university buildings, which were published in 1690. He was assisted by several people, including Michael Burghers (1647/8–1724) who followed him as the engraver at the University of Oxford, and apparently engraved several of the plates in the diary (see note on page 73). It was whilst doing an engraving of King's College Chapel in Cambridge that Loggan was supposed to have damaged his eyesight—a shame considering the splendour of the building. He died in 1692, with considerable debts despite a successful career.

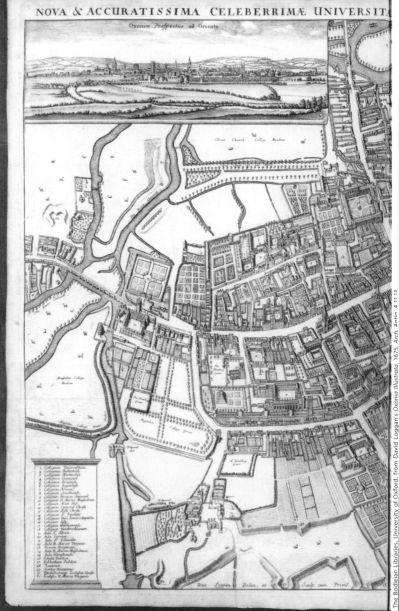

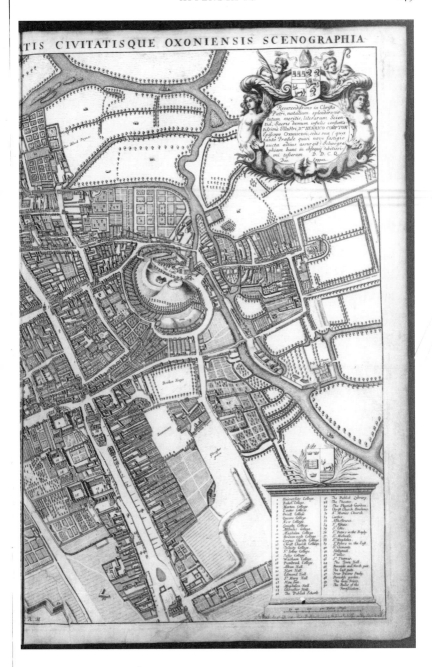

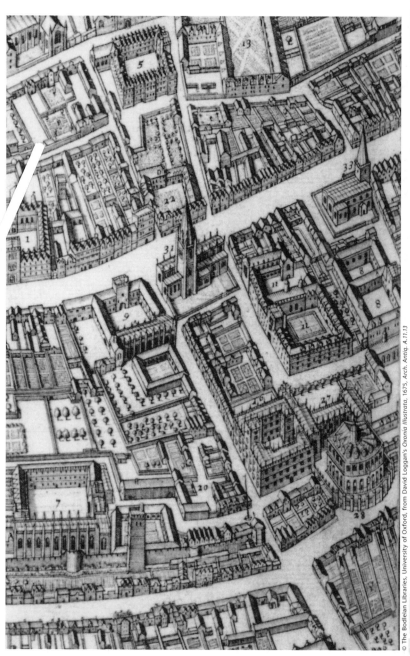

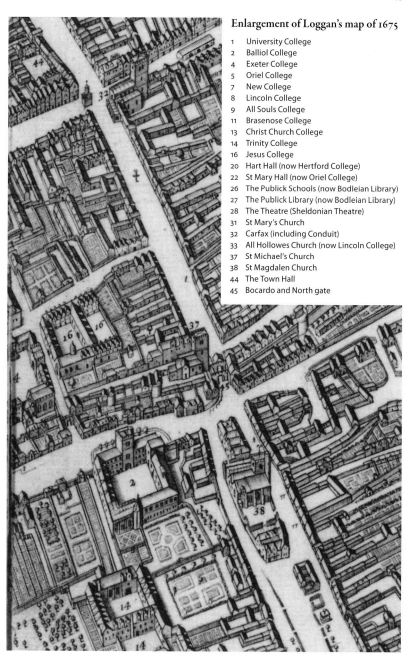

Enlargement of Loggan's map of 1675

1 University College
2 Balliol College
4 Exeter College
5 Oriel College
7 New College
8 Lincoln College
9 All Souls College
11 Brasenose College
13 Christ Church College
14 Trinity College
16 Jesus College
20 Hart Hall (now Hertford College)
22 St Mary Hall (now Oriel College)
26 The Publick Schools (now Bodleian Library)
27 The Publick Library (now Bodleian Library)
28 The Theatre (Sheldonian Theatre)
31 St Mary's Church
32 Carfax (including Conduit)
33 All Hollowes Church (now Lincoln College)
37 St Michael's Church
38 St Magdalen Church
44 The Town Hall
45 Bocardo and North gate

SOUTH

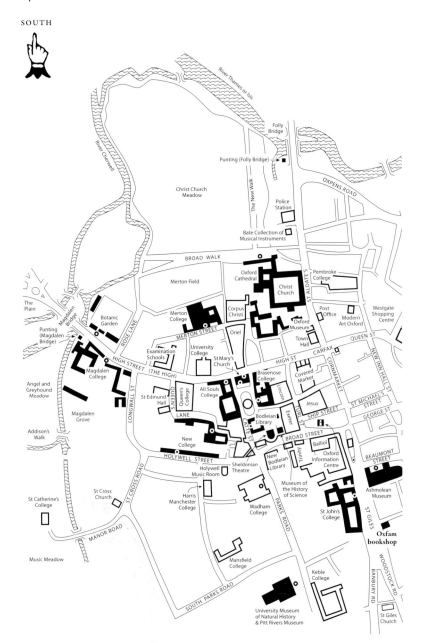

Oxford

A map of Oxford as it is today, with well-known buildings shown in black. A close-up of this map is shown on the following pages. Please note that as David Loggan's map has south at the top, this map follows the same convention to make it easier to compare one to the other. Most maps today have north at the top.

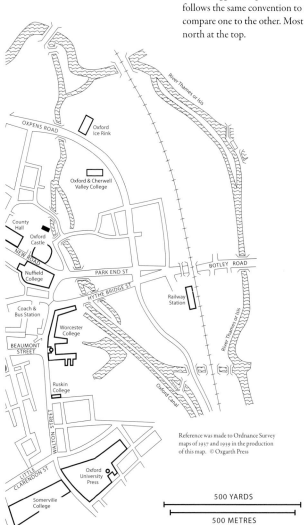

River Thames or Isis

OXPENS ROAD

Oxford Ice Rink

Oxford & Cherwell Valley College

County Hall

Oxford Castle

NEW ROAD

Nuffield College

PARK END ST

BOTLEY ROAD

HYTHE BRIDGE ST

Railway Station

Coach & Bus Station

Worcester College

BEAUMONT STREET

River Thames or Isis

Ruskin College

Oxford Canal

WALTON STREET

Reference was made to Ordnance Survey maps of 1937 and 1939 in the production of this map. © Oxgarth Press

LITTLE CLARENDON ST

Oxford University Press

Somerville College

500 YARDS

500 METRES

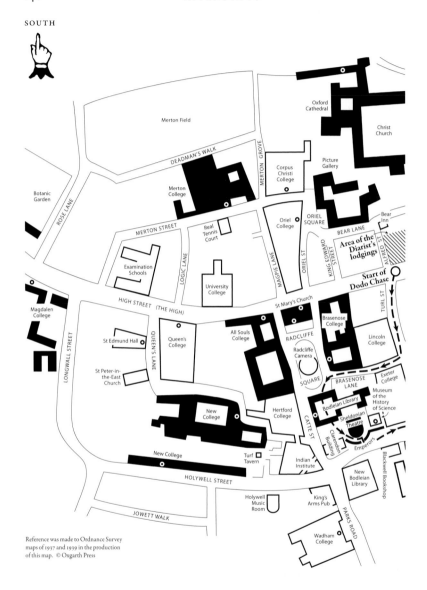

SOUTH

Merton Field

Oxford Cathedral

Christ Church

DEADMAN'S WALK

MERTON GROVE

Corpus Christi College

Picture Gallery

Botanic Garden

ROSE LANE

Merton College

Oriel College

ORIEL SQUARE

Bear Inn

MERTON STREET

Real Tennis Court

BEAR LANE

Area of the Diarist's lodgings

LOGIC LANE

MAGPIE LANE

ORIEL ST

KING EDWARD STREET

ALFRED ST

Examination Schools

University College

Start of Dodo Chase

TURL ST

HIGH STREET (THE HIGH)

St Mary's Church

Magdalen College

LONGWALL STREET

St Edmund Hall

Queen's College

QUEEN'S LANE

All Souls College

RADCLIFFE

Brasenose College

Lincoln College

St Peter-in-the-East Church

Radcliffe Camera

SQUARE

BRASENOSE LANE

Exeter College

Museum of the History of Science

New College

Hertford College

CATTE ST

Bodleian Library

Sheldonian Theatre

Clarendon Building

Emperors

Blackwell Bookshop

New College

Turf Tavern

Indian Institute

New Bodleian Library

HOLYWELL STREET

PARKS ROAD

Holywell Music Room

King's Arms Pub

JOWETT WALK

Wadham College

Reference was made to Ordnance Survey maps of 1937 and 1939 in the production of this map. © Oxgarth Press

200 METRES

200 YARDS

City Centre

The Diarist's lodgings were somewhere off the High Street, near to Carfax. A series of dashes show the probable route of the diarist as he chased after the dodo. At the bottom of this page is the Oxfam bookshop, where the diary was purchased.

EPILOGUE

―――――――

At the last moment before sending this book
to be printed, it has been possible to add this page.
Unfortunately, we must apologize, as the diary
has been tragically lost.

A dog appeared from nowhere
and ran off with it.

If any reader has come across a black and
white mongrel, last seen disappearing northwards
up St Giles, Oxford, please could they contact
the publisher. It had one ear, a slight limp,
a profusely studded collar, and
a book in its jaws.